There was silence for such a long time Kennedy wondered if there was a problem with Carl's antique cell phone. Finally, Rose asked, "And so what happens if you get pregnant, and you're too young to actually have a baby?"

Defying all laws of inertia, the acceleration of Kennedy's heart rate crashed to a halt like a car plowing into a brick wall. "What do you mean?"

"Like, what if you're too young but you still get pregnant?"

"How young?" Kennedy spoke both words clearly and slowly, as if rushing might drive the timid voice away for good.

"Like thirteen."

Praise for *Unplanned*
by Alana Terry

"Deals with **one of the most difficult situations a pregnancy center could ever face**. The message is **powerful** and the story-telling **compelling**." ~ William Donovan, *Executive Director Anchorage Community Pregnancy Center*

"Alana Terry does an amazing job tackling a very **sensitive subject from the mother's perspective**." ~ Pamela McDonald, *Director Okanogan CareNet Pregnancy Center*

"**Thought-provoking** and intense ... Shows **different sides of the abortion argument**." ~ Sharee Stover, *Wordy Nerdy*

"Alana has a way of sharing the gospel **without being preachy**." ~ Phyllis Sather, *Purposeful Planning*

Note: The views of the characters in this novel do not necessarily reflect the views of the author.

Unplanned
Copyright © 2015 Alana Terry
9781941735244
April, 2015

Cover design by Damonza.

www.alanaterry.com

Unplanned

a novel by Alana Terry

"For you created my inmost being.
You knit me together in my mother's womb.
I praise you because I am fearfully and wonderfully made."

Psalm 139:13-14

CHAPTER 1

"You look really familiar. Did you go to Harvard?"

Kennedy glanced up from her reading at the red-haired stranger. "I'm there now. Are you?"

"I was." He moved to the seat next to her on the subway and furrowed his brow. "Graduated two years ago. Were we in the same class together maybe? I was a journalism major."

Kennedy had at least another hundred pages of Dostoevsky to finish by the end of the weekend, reading she couldn't get done chitchatting on the T with former journalism students. "No, this is my first year."

He situated his leather case on his lap. It looked heavy. "I swear I've seen you before. Did you grow up around here?"

She lowered her book but kept it open to the right page. "No, I've been in China for the past ten years." She thought about her dad's paranoia, how he still reminded her from a dozen time zones away to stay wary of strangers.

"China?" The journalist leaned forward. "What part?"

Kennedy had lost track of the times she had been asked that by Americans who wouldn't know where to look for Beijing on a map. Sometimes, she took pity and said she lived near the Chinese-North Korean border. Other times, she gave the actual name of the city or province and watched their eyes go blank while they nodded absently. That was usually the tactic she employed when she didn't particularly feel like talking.

"Jilin Province," she answered, picking up her book again.

The man's eyes grew wide. "Really? Were you near Longjing by any chance?"

Kennedy couldn't tell which impressed her more, the journalist's familiarity with the Chinese geography or his accent-free pronunciation. When she left Yanji at summer's end, she couldn't wait to get "home" to the States. There wasn't anything for her to miss back in China. But when she got to campus and saw how different most of her classmates were, she realized how wrong she had been. She actually carved time out of her studies last month to go to the Asian-American Students' first meeting, but she was the only white girl there and never went back.

"We actually lived in Yanji," she told him.

The man nodded in apparent recognition. "I spent a year

2

abroad in Longjing. I'm going back in a few months." He patted the case on his lap. A camera, maybe? "Working on my first international documentary."

The T's automated announcer called out the name of Kennedy's stop. She stood and gave him a wave and a little Americanized half bow. "I've got to go, but good luck with that documentary."

"Yeah, good luck in school," he managed to reply before Kennedy stepped onto the platform and hurried to the escalators, checking the time on her cell phone.

She adjusted her book bag when she emerged from the subway station. It was one of the chilliest days she could remember since arriving back in the States. The air was crisp and invigorating, and she walked with brisk steps. What a strange coincidence to meet someone so familiar with her home region. She thought about mentioning it to her parents when they talked next. Then again, her dad would probably reprove her for divulging even that amount of personal information. Oh well. Kennedy was on her own now, and she couldn't waste her life scurrying from every shadow. Besides, Cambridge was a safe town with a public transportation system that was infinitely easier to grasp than the one back in Yanji. She didn't venture off campus much, but when she did, she never felt insecure. She pitied folks

3

like her dad who lived their lives in constant terror. Why couldn't he be a little more trusting of people?

A burst of leaves fluttered to the pavement, and she quickened her step. She wasn't late, not yet, but she walked fast enough that it would have impressed an Olympic speed-walker. She hadn't seen her childhood pastor in years. His would be the first familiar face she saw since arriving back in the States, and she was anxious to catch up with him.

When Carl emailed her a few weeks ago, she was thrilled at the prospect of getting together. Finding the time to do so was a little more difficult. At least his new center was only a few hops away from campus on the Red Line — a convenient coincidence. *Not coincidence.* She could almost hear Carl correct her in his melodious bass voice that would make James Earl Jones drool with envy. *Providence.*

Either way, she was excited to see him. She still remembered his wife Sandy, her Sunday school teacher for years and years, and the one who let Kennedy practice time and time again on her hair until she perfected the art of French braiding.

She saw the dark green sign for the pregnancy center, felt the smile spread across her face, and swung open the door. A little bell announced her arrival. The room was empty except for the fumes of day-old paint.

"Hello?" She held her breath. Was anybody even here?

"Kennedy!" Carl Lindgren bustled out of a back office, arms extended jovially. "You made it." His voice reverberated off the walls. He grabbed both her arms to draw her in for a rib-crushing bear hug. "You sure have grown since you were little."

"It's great to see you." She didn't have to feign her enthusiasm. The past two months had been a whirlwind of college orientations, lectures, homework, and already two all-nighters. Seeing Carl's face was like stepping into a sauna in the middle of winter. The turpentine vapor intermingled with the scent of his shirt, a combination of barbecue, home-cooking, and after-shave that almost matched her father's.

"When your family left for China, you were such a little thing." He held his hand at the level of his waist. "Now look at you. All grown up, off on your own."

Kennedy laughed. *On her own* meant she lived in a dorm with a theater-major roommate from Alaska, whose entire education — from what Kennedy could tell — consisted of playing computer games, attending rehearsals, and reading an occasional play. Kennedy, on the other hand, was so busy with her pre-med studies and literature classes that she hadn't yet experienced any of the so-called "freedoms" supposed to come with college life.

Carl gave her a quick tour of the new pregnancy center, which in reality was only slightly larger than Kennedy's dorm room. There was a main waiting area still wanting furniture, a back office, and a single room tucked in the corner. "Here's where we do the counseling sessions, and that door there opens to a little bathroom stall."

"It's really nice," Kennedy stated automatically, while her head threatened to lift right off her shoulders because of the fumes.

Carl's cheeks widened into one of his chipmunk-style grins. "Well, it's something. We'll still have to send folks to the Boston campus for ultrasounds until we get a bigger place, but it's a start. Oh." His eyes lit up. "Wait until you see what Sandy rigged up for us."

"How's Sandy doing these days?" Kennedy followed Carl to his little office, the only room with any sort of décor. A golden placard marked the territory as the Executive Director's, and the desk was already cluttered with paperwork and framed pictures of fat, cherubic toddlers. A few finger-painted masterpieces were taped to the wall, along with a crayon drawing on construction paper that read *I love Grandpa.*

Carl shuffled from side to side as he bustled around behind his desk. "You know Sandy," he said with a beam.

"She's been as busy as ever getting this place ready to open, doing her grandma thing three days a week, overseeing all of the children's ministry volunteers at St. Margaret's." He narrowed his eyes for a moment, but they didn't lose their playful twinkle. "You know, I haven't seen you at church, young lady."

Kennedy had anticipated the remark and was ready with her excuse. "It's just really busy with schoolwork and all, and it's hard not having a car of my own."

"I won't say anything to your father." Carl winked. "But you know my Sandy. You give her a call on Saturday night, and she'll be sure to find you a ride for Sunday morning. Be sure to get her number from me before you leave. Or if you like taking the T, we're right off the Red Line, Davis stop. Just another fifteen-minute walk from here, really." He frowned. "But maybe you shouldn't be walking that far alone."

Kennedy tried not to roll her eyes. Had he been talking to her dad? She wasn't ready to make any promises about coming to church, but she'd try finding time soon. It had been years since she had participated in an American service. She was a little nervous she might have forgotten something important. The kind of worship she was used to in China was quite different.

"By the way," Carl went on, "Sandy told me specifically to tell you she wants to take you out for coffee sometime soon." He gestured to the entrance of his office. "And if you shut the door, you can see her newest piece of art."

On the wall hung a large, poster-sized calendar. Even though it was obviously made by hand, the printing was impeccable and the lines for each date were as rigid as a surgeon's scalpel. Inside every box were color-coded sections marked *Morning Volunteer*, *Afternoon Volunteer*, and *Hotline Receptionist*. Kennedy almost remarked that Carl's wife must have a lot of extra time on her hands, but then she noticed Sandy was listed as the morning volunteer for all but two days that month and was penned in for half of the afternoon shifts as well.

Carl spread out his hands. "We definitely are asking God for more workers. But the good news is you can have first pick of whatever shift you want to volunteer."

Kennedy pursed her lips together and reminded herself that her job was to keep up her GPA, not to make everyone around her happy. "Yeah, well, I've been thinking since I got your email, and I just don't know if I can make that kind of time commitment." She didn't want to admit that adjusting to life back in the States was taking about the same amount of mental acuity as keeping up with her chem lab and its

8

monstrous piles of work. Her mind had been reeling ever since she landed at Logan Airport. American slang she had never heard in China, fads that seemed to upgrade themselves once a week or more ... She hardly had time to keep up her grades, let alone give herself room to acculturate back to life in the States. If she jumped into volunteer work right now, she'd probably get so confused she'd start speaking to the clients in Korean or give some poor woman a lecture on chemical ionization when she was supposed to ask her to pee in a cup.

Carl's smile wilted for a short second, and his shoulders sank toward the floor while his chest deflated. "I understand. It's been a long time since my college days." His eyes twinkled once again, and he chuckled. "Compared to pastoring a church, starting up a pregnancy center satellite, and chasing around a bunch of grandkids, it sounds like a breeze." He was talking quietly, almost under his breath. "No utility bills, no board meetings ..." His head snapped up when his eyes met Kennedy's. "Never mind. I want you to know I get it. You're busy." He looked at the color-coded calendar, where his wife's was the only name on record. He smacked his lips. "Well, we'll be having our new center kick-off dinner Thursday night. That's where we're hoping to get most of our volunteers from, anyway."

Shame heated up Kennedy's core. "I didn't mean I couldn't help at all." She wouldn't have bothered taking the T all the way to the new center just to tell him that. "I'd love to be involved when I can. I was thinking as a substitute. Or maybe I could come help with paperwork or something on the weekends. I don't really know what you need."

"We need everything," Carl sighed. He stared at the calendar. When a little tinny rendition of *Brahms' Lullaby* rang out, his eyes widened, and he thrust his hands into his pants pockets. "That's the hotline phone." His face flushed and he patted his chest. "I don't have voicemail set up yet. I gotta answer it." The ringtone was almost through the first strain when he finally pulled out a small, black cell phone from his shirt pocket and promptly dropped it on the ground. His head nearly bonked Kennedy's when they both reached down to grab it. Finally, he picked it up and punched the button.

"Cambridge Community Pregnancy Center," he answered breathlessly.

Kennedy wondered if the caller could hear how flustered he was. A second later, he let out a sigh, and the vein that had threatened to pop its way out of his forehead relaxed a little.

"Oh. Hi, Sugar. I didn't know it was you. Why didn't you call me on … Oh, I must have turned it to silent … No, it's just that I thought it was a client. I'm here with Kennedy, you know, Roger Stern's girl. She's at Harvard now ... Of course I already told you that, but I didn't know if you would remember ... Yeah, I'll pick some up on my way home ... No, I'm not mad. I just thought we had our first call ... Ok, I love you, too, babe. ... Yup." Carl pulled his glasses down a little on his nose and squinted at the phone. He scratched his cheek. "Now how do I turn it off from my end?"

He glanced up at Kennedy, and another flush crept across his dark brown skin for a second. "This is our new hotline phone." He held up the contraption as if presenting evidence and then squinted at it one more time over his lenses. "I still haven't figured out how it works. They have these things over in China?"

Kennedy tried to keep herself from rolling her eyes. "Yeah." Why did everyone assume she was a transplant from the dark ages?

Carl weaved his way around some boxes to get behind his desk. "Well, we just started advertising for the pregnancy center on the radio yesterday. That means we could get a call on here any time, day or night. Sandy's busy, and I'm, well, I'm tied up with other things." He nearly dropped the phone again as his large hands struggled to slip it back into his pocket. "So maybe you could be our phone girl?"

He glanced up at her nervously.

Before Kennedy could say anything, Carl hurried on, "Of course, school has got to come first. Your dad told me about your program, by the way, how you're already accepted into the …"

"You just need someone to answer calls?" Kennedy interrupted.

"That's all. The clinic itself is only open on a part-time basis — at least until we get more volunteers to keep it staffed. But we want people to be able to get in touch with us whenever they need." His eyes widened imploringly. "Would you? At least some of the time?"

Kennedy cast a glance at all the empty slots left on the wall calendar. How hard could it be to answer a cell phone every once in a while? "Sure. I can do that."

Carl's breath rushed out in a loud hiss before another smile broadened his face. "You're an angel." He took her by both shoulders and pulled her in for a quick hug. Then fiddling with his pocket, he managed to get the phone out without dropping it and pressed it in Kennedy's hand. "And if I know Sandy, she's going to want to know what kind of cookies you like most. She's convinced any college student who's not living at home must be starving." He passed her a pad of purple Post-it notes. "So you write down your address

12

here, then just you wait if she doesn't show up at your dorm with a whole platter of them. Better write down what kind you like, too."

Kennedy jotted down her name and room number. "I'll eat anything home-baked."

Carl slammed the note onto his desk and clasped his hands together. "You have no idea how much of a burden you just lifted from me. So you'll take the phone this weekend? You don't have any plans, do you? No dates?"

Kennedy couldn't be sure, but she thought she saw him wink. "Nothing at all. Just lab reports."

"Perfect!" Carl remarked. It wasn't exactly the same reaction Kennedy had when she thought about her twelve-page write-up she'd be working on. He picked up a pink pen, squinted at the calendar, and traded it for a turquoise one. "See how proud Sandy would be of me for using her color system?" He made his way to the wall calendar and wrote Kennedy's name next to *Hotline Receptionist* for the weekend. "Oh, do you want me to teach you how to use it?"

Kennedy glanced at the model and guessed it was more ancient than the artifact her dad carried around back in Yanji. "I'm sure I can figure it out."

Carl insisted on showing her anyway, even though it was Kennedy who did most of the teaching as well as a decent amount of correcting. When they were done, she slipped the cell into the front zipper of her backpack. "So what do I do if I actually get a call?"

He adjusted his glasses once more. "Well, I think all you have to do is press that green button and ..."

"No, I mean, what am I supposed to say? What kind of calls am I going to get?"

Carl had been bustling about, apparently without aim, but now froze completely. "You've never done crisis pregnancy ministry before, have you?"

She shook her head.

He sat down with a loud sigh and gestured for Kennedy to take the miniature recliner along the wall. For a moment, he stared in silence, but then his eyes grew wide and his face brightened. "We got some training brochures just yesterday in the mail." Carl rummaged through some piles on his desk. "And if you come back next week, I can get you a few of the videos we use for training back at the Boston campus. That's where we're getting most of our materials from, you know."

Kennedy nodded. If she could get straight A's her senior year of high school while taking four AP classes, she figured she could handle answering a cell phone. She knew a passing amount of information about pregnancy centers. Her dad was quite passionate about the pro-life movement, and she had vague memories of her mother going to fancy fundraising teas when they still lived in the States. Abortion was a big problem in China with its one-child policy, and she heard her parents sometimes talk about forced abortions in North Korea as well.

Something buzzed, and Carl jumped to his feet, wincing when he banged his knee against the desk. With a focus that reminded Kennedy of her childhood schnauzer looking for his tennis ball, Carl patted himself down until he pulled out the source of buzzing from his pocket.

"Rats, I'm running late." He tapped at his phone with his beefy finger several times before he finally silenced the alarm. "I completely forgot. We have a prayer meeting for the St. Margaret's staff. I didn't even think of that when I was emailing you. I just can't seem to keep track of my schedule these days." He squinted as he stared at his screen, his brow wrinkled in consternation. "Kennedy, I'm sorry to up and leave so fast. Can I drop you off on campus on my way?"

Kennedy glanced at the clock on the wall. She was done with classes for the week and didn't have any plans except for finishing that lab report and catching up on some of her reading. "I don't mind taking the T."

"Well, since there's not time anymore for a proper training, you can give me the phone back. We can get you those brochures and have you come in and watch a few videos next week. If you're not too busy," he added hastily as he pulled a clanging ring of keys out of his top drawer.

"I don't mind taking the phone for the weekend." Kennedy saw the tight worry lines above Carl's eyes fade into his forehead, and she knew she had made the right decision.

He frowned for a second as he zipped up his windbreaker. "If you're sure you're comfortable. You can bring it back to me at church on Sunday so you won't have to carry it around during the week. Besides, that means you don't have an excuse to miss services. Oh, I forgot to give you Sandy's number in case you need a ride."

He reached down for a pen from a *#1 Grandpa* mug on his desk before Kennedy held up her hand. "That's all right. I can look up her number from caller ID."

He froze for a moment, his eyes wide. "You can do that?" He shook his head and shrugged. "All right, well, are you sure you're comfortable with the phone then? I didn't mean to spring it on you so fast and then just throw you to the wolves."

Kennedy laughed as she followed him out his office. "It's only for two days. What could be so hard about that?"

CHAPTER 2

Kennedy loved her literature courses because all that reading gave her a perfect and acceptable reason to procrastinate from math and science for a while. After she got back to campus, she hurried through a round of calculus problems to prepare for a test next Tuesday, then she took her already worn copy of *Crime and Punishment* and headed to the student union. Since it was a Friday evening, the cafeteria was pretty empty, but Kennedy wouldn't regret spending some time alone.

She picked at her vegetarian pasta while she read Dostoevsky's scene about a crazed murderer giving alms to a drunkard's destitute family. So far, she was enjoying her Russian literature class even more than she thought she would. There was something about the way the writers described the world, something that immediately engaged her emotions and her spirit. They didn't shy away from depicting human suffering in all its awful hues, but there was an underlying hope and beauty, too. After living in Yanji and walking its alleys overrun by homeless vagabonds, after spending time with the North Korean refugees her parents sheltered from the Chinese police, Kennedy appreciated the depth she found in the Russian works she read.

She turned the page, accidentally smudging a little salad dressing on the corner, when someone plopped a beige tray across from her on the table. "Hey, you."

She glanced up when she heard the familiar accent, her lips spreading in a ready smile.

"Is that all you're eating today?" her lab partner asked, eyeing her plate. Reuben sat down in front of his rice and beans, two slices of pizza, a cup of Jell-O, a bag of chips, and two cans of Coke.

Kennedy still had at least three hours' worth of reading to finish before her class next Monday, but she slipped a napkin between the pages and welcomed the intrusion. Her eyes were so scratchy she felt as though her eyelids were made of steel wool. With the late nights and excessive reading, her contacts were constantly dried out. She hadn't found the time to call her dad to ask him for a refill prescription, either. The time difference combined with her dad's long hours at his printing office made him tricky to contact. She blinked a few times and tried not to rub her eyes as she stared at Reuben's plate.

"Hungry?" she teased.

His mouth was already full with his first bites of rice and beans. He and Kennedy had been in the same small group during their first-year orientation. He was from Kenya, and they quickly discovered they faced some of the same challenges adjusting to life in the States. When they saw each other on the first day of chemistry lab, they silently agreed to stick together and make sure neither became one of Harvard's pre-med dropout statistics.

"Wichaeading?" Reuben mumbled through a mouthful of pizza. When Kennedy wrinkled her nose at him, he swallowed noisily and asked again, "What're you reading?"

"*Crime and Punishment*," she answered, showing him the cover. "It's for my Russian lit class." Reuben was already hacking at his Jell-O with a spork, and Kennedy guessed it would be her job to hold up the conversation for a while. "It's about a young man who decides to kill this old lady ..."

"Pwnvroker," he muttered.

Kennedy squinted while she tried to translate, and then she nodded. "The pawnbroker. Right. So, you've read it?"

Reuben held up two fingers. Kennedy was impressed. She enjoyed a spy or thriller novel as much as the classics she read for class, but even when she found a book she liked, she hardly re-read anything. There wasn't enough time.

Reuben's meal was half eaten in a matter of minutes, which allowed him to keep up a more regular conversation. He told Kennedy about the other books by Dostoevsky he had read, and they talked literature until both their plates were empty. After a quiet burp, Reuben leaned back in his chair with a grin.

"So, any exciting weekend plans?" Reuben sipped his Coke. He was always so easy to talk to, whether he was discussing acid-base reactions or telling her about growing up in Kenya in a family with seven sisters. He couldn't even count all his nephews and nieces on his ten fingers anymore, but he gave Kennedy detailed reports about them and their activities nearly every time he saw her.

"Not really," Kennedy answered. She wondered how he always remained so relaxed. He hadn't stressed about anything yet, at least not that she had seen. Between sips of Coke, Reuben cocked his head to the side and grinned at her until she finally had to ask what he was thinking about.

"Just wondering what my sisters would say if they met you."

She crossed her arms. "Oh, yeah?" she smirked. "And what would they say?"

Reuben kept a deadpan expression. "Stressed."

They both laughed.

"So when are you meeting me to work on our lab?" he asked.

She thought about her schedule. "Tomorrow good?"

Reuben shook his head. "No, I'll be busy."

Kennedy almost asked what he would be doing, but there was something in his closed posture that made her change her mind. That was the funny thing about Reuben. She figured it must be some kind of cultural thing she wasn't used to yet. He was gregarious and outgoing, but he could close up like a clam without any provocation and then be right back to his charming self again a few seconds later.

"What about Sunday?" she suggested after the crease in his brow eased up. She glanced at her backpack. What was she forgetting? That's right. Carl. "Oh, it would have to be in the afternoon. I told an old family friend I'd go to his church this Sunday." She glanced at Reuben, trying to gauge his present mood. "Do you want to come with me?"

Never hurts to ask, right?

She didn't know whether he would jump up and start singing like he did after they both aced their first chemistry test or if he would get sullen and silent as if she had intentionally offended him. Reuben's face turned thoughtful, but at least he wasn't scowling. "I'm not much of a churchgoer," he finally remarked.

"First time for everything," she tried. "What about your family? Are they religious?"

Reuben let out a little chuckle. "Oh, we're religious all right. Christians through and through. I'm just, well, I'm not one for churches, that's all."

Brahms' Lullaby interrupted their conversation, and Kennedy held up her finger. "Sorry, I need to get that." She felt Reuben staring at her while she pulled out the hotline phone. The call came from a blocked number. She turned her body away slightly so Reuben didn't have to hear the entire conversation and pressed the green button. "Cambridge Pregnancy Center." That was the right name, wasn't it?

"Hello?" The voice was so quiet and mouse-like Kennedy could almost feel the hairs in her ear straining to grasp as much of the faint sound as they could. She stood up. Why hadn't she let Carl explain to her what she was supposed to do when she got a call?

"Hi. You've reached the Cambridge Pregnancy Center." Kennedy waited for a response. Did the caller hang up?

Nothing.

"Are you still there?" Kennedy winced and kicked herself for sounding rude. She was here to be a good listener, right? She looked at the screen to make sure the call was still connected.

"I'm here." The voice was young. Feathery, like wispy little egg whites floating in a bowl of egg drop soup. When Kennedy offered to take the hotline calls, she pictured herself talking to college co-eds or frazzled single moms. Not little girls.

"Can I help you?" What else was she supposed to say? And why in the world had she taken the job before at least reading one of Carl's silly training brochures?

"I just had a question." She wasn't exactly whispering. It sounded as if her body was so tiny and fragile she couldn't spare an ounce more breath to make herself heard.

Kennedy held up her finger to tell Reuben she'd return in a minute and hurried to the corner of the student union. "Sure. What's your name?"

There was a pause. Had Kennedy scared her away?

"Rose."

"All right, Rose. Ask me anything."

Kennedy waited for another silent eternity before the voice asked, "Do abortions hurt?"

Of course, that would be the first question. Not the clinic's hours, although Kennedy didn't even know that much. She tried to remember some of the arguments she heard her dad spout off when he went on one of his anti-abortion spiels.

"Well, the brain is fully functional very early on ..." Was it two months? Three months? She had never bothered to memorize the statistics. "And there are ultrasounds that lead us to believe that yes, babies can experience pain during an abortion." Is that what Carl would want her to say? Was she getting any of her facts right? For a minute, she thought about looking up the phone number for Carl's wife. Sandy would definitely be a better resource in this situation, but the phone model was so old she couldn't pull up the number without disconnecting the call. Hadn't Carl heard of modern technology?

The voice made a little gurgling sound that might have been a stifled cry or else a miniature cough. "No, I mean, does it hurt *you*."

"Oh." Kennedy had never thought about that before. All the pro-life arguments she heard growing up focused on the baby, not the mother. "Well, I know it's a complicated procedure. There are probably risks involved ..." If she were back in her room, she could Google the question and have an answer in a second or two. Maybe she should head back there now. The thought of Willow, her feminist roommate, listening in to the call might have been amusing if Kennedy's internal viscera weren't quivering so much. She shut her eyes. She had to take charge of the conversation. "So, are you considering an abortion? Is that why you're asking?"

Too direct.

"No. I'm calling for a friend. That's all. She was just wondering."

Nice job, Kennedy chided herself. "And how old is your friend?" She tried to make her tone sound trustworthy, inviting. She had no idea if she was succeeding or not because her pulse roared in her ear, making it nearly impossible to hear anything else.

"She's thirteen." It felt like Kennedy's whole abdominal floor dropped several feet to the ground at terminal velocity. "I mean eighteen," the voice corrected. "She's eighteen and already out of school."

Kennedy's heart accelerated so fast her pulse felt like a long, continuous flutter. *Thirteen?* "And so your friend is thinking about an abortion?"

"Well, she just wanted some information, really. Like if it hurts a lot or not."

"I see." Kennedy shot up a wordless prayer to heaven, a silent plea for help that rose from her spirit before she had time to translate it into human language. "Well, if your friend wants to stop by the pregnancy center, we're open again on Monday ..."

"I don't know if her parents will let her come in."

"Well, you certainly can't make her. But if you talk to her, let her know there are nice people there who really do want to help. They can answer all the questions she has and give her the information she needs."

"You guys are Christians, right?"

Kennedy was pacing now, because the more she moved her legs, the less her abdominal muscles quivered. "Yes, the pregnancy center is run by Christians. But you don't have to be a Christian to get help there," she added quickly.

There was silence for such a long time Kennedy wondered if there was a problem with Carl's antique cell phone. Finally, Rose asked, "And so what happens if you get pregnant, and you're too young to actually have a baby?"

Defying all laws of inertia, the acceleration of Kennedy's heart rate crashed to a halt like a car plowing into a brick wall. "What do you mean?"

"Like, what if you're too young but you still get pregnant?"

"How young?" Kennedy spoke both words clearly and slowly, as if rushing might drive the timid voice away for good.

"Like thirteen."

Kennedy paused. She was pretty sure Carl's training

would have some sort of method, some sort of guidelines for a situation like this. But she had nothing to go on but intuition. Intuition that at this point was sending ripples of foreboding creeping up her spine until they wormed in and settled at the base of her neck. "Are you asking because you might be pregnant?" The question itself made her dizzy, as if speaking the words aloud could send her head into some kind of tailspin.

"Yeah."

The adrenaline that had flooded Kennedy's entire nervous system seeped out of her body in a single moment, dissipating out of each pore. She leaned against the wall and reminded herself that her job was to help and encourage the caller, not have some sort of fainting dizzy spell in the middle of the student union.

"And you're how old?" She braced herself for the answer she knew was coming.

"Thirteen."

Now what? Instinct demanded Kennedy find out where the girl lived, who her parents were. Compassion welled up in her core, urging her to find this child and … and what? What could she do?

"Do you know about how long ago you might have gotten pregnant?" Kennedy scolded herself. Wasn't there a more discreet way to ask something like that?

"Five months."

Kennedy felt her eyes grow wide. "Does your family know?" She thought about what she had been like at thirteen. Obsessed with horses, daydreaming about NASA, content to giggle with her girlfriends about which boys at school were the cutest. But pregnant?

"I can't tell them," Rose whispered.

Kennedy wished she had written down Sandy's phone number. What did Kennedy know about pregnancy? Nothing. In fact Reuben with his seven sisters probably knew more about childbearing than she did.

Think, Kennedy. Thirteen-year-old tells you she's five months pregnant. What do you do?

"Have you been to a doctor yet?"

"No. I just took one of those tests you pee on." Rose's voice was too small to hold so much fear.

Nervous energy raced up and down Kennedy's limbs. She had to find something to do. "Maybe we should make you an appointment at the pregnancy center. Would that be ok?"

"I don't have any way to get there." Another brick wall. What would Carl do?

"All right, what about your school counselor? Could you make an appointment with them?"

"I'm homeschooled."

A roar of frustration crept up to the base of Kennedy's larynx, where she cut it off by clenching her throat muscles. "What about your boyfriend?" she finally asked. "Could his family maybe help you out? Could they give you a ride to the center? We really want to help you."

Did Rose understand? Did she guess that Kennedy's leg muscles were poised, ready to run out the door the moment she discovered something she could do, some way she could assist?

"I don't have a boyfriend."

A horrible, nagging dread nibbled the inside of Kennedy's gut. She asked her next inevitable question slowly, almost against her will. "How are you pregnant, then?"

A little sharp breath, the sound a startled animal might make when it notices its prey. A fear-drenched whisper. "I think it's my dad ... I gotta go."

"No, wait!" Kennedy nearly shouted into the phone, but Rose had already hung up.

CHAPTER 3

"No, I can't calm down." Kennedy didn't mean to snap, but after the third or fourth time Reuben made the suggestion, she was ready to gouge his eyes out. Kennedy was pacing in front of some benches outside the student union while Reuben did his best to listen. "I mean, she might not have meant her dad is the dad, right?"

"I don't know." Reuben shrugged. "I wasn't on the phone."

Kennedy replayed those last few words in her mind. She could hear Rose's voice, clear as a tiny glass beaker. Saturated with fear. *I think it's my dad ... I gotta go.* Did that mean her dad was the father of the baby? Or maybe her dad was coming, and she didn't want him to catch her on the phone. Even so, there were still troubling questions without any answers. How does a thirteen-year-old girl get pregnant if she doesn't have a boyfriend?

"Why did she hang up so quick?" Kennedy asked the air.

Reuben picked his tooth. "Maybe it was time for dinner."

She whipped her head around to face him. "I don't think it's something to joke about."

He held up his hands in a position of surrender.

Kennedy hoped he knew she wasn't really mad at him. She eyed the stupid phone. "Anyway, I better call the director." She hated running to Carl her very first night on the job, but there really wasn't anything else to do. "I'll see you later." She started walking toward her dorm, but Reuben ran up behind and reached for her shoulder.

"Wait, when are we going to work on the paper for chem lab, then?"

"I don't know." How could she think about some report while there was some traumatized little girl out there? "Let's just meet in the library Sunday afternoon."

"When? Two?"

Kennedy was hardly listening. "All right. Fine."

She turned once more, only to hear Reuben call after her, "And don't stay up all night worrying. These things work themselves out." She gave him a brief wave, discarded his last words which were about as helpful as a lobotomy, and pushed all thoughts of Reuben and lab write-ups aside. She glanced down at the phone, and her fingers trembled so much it took her three tries before the call went through. Whenever she clenched her ab muscles to keep them from quivering, the tremors relocated all the way up to her teeth and sent them chattering noisily. She took a deep breath, hoping the phone would mask the choppiness in her voice. She had been so impatient to talk to Carl she hadn't thought about what she would do if nobody answered at all. By the fifth ring, her shivering was so violent she sat down on a bench but hopped right back up again since her muscles refused to relax.

"Hello?" At the sound of Carl's voice, relief flooded Kennedy's whole body and seeped into each individual cell.

"Carl, it's Kennedy. I just got off the hotline phone."

"Oh, really? That was even faster than I expected."

She hated to squash his enthusiasm, but she had no energy left for pleasantries or small talk. She summarized the call and waited for Carl to comment.

"So, you think the father might be ..."

"She didn't say so," Kennedy hurried to explain, as if that one simple statement could negate all her horrific suspicions. "But on the other hand ..."

"A thirteen-year-old without a boyfriend ..." Carl mumbled. "It doesn't necessarily have to be her dad." His voice held the same futile optimism Kennedy had been trying to cling to.

"That's true," she agreed.

"But it does have to be somebody."

"Right."

"Do you think it'd be a good idea to call her back?" Carl suggested.

"It was a blocked number. I couldn't even if I wanted."

He let out a huge breath of air. "We better report this, just in case."

"Report to who?" Kennedy shivered. It was warm when she dressed that morning. Now she wished she had layered up. It wasn't sunset yet, but the night was freezing.

"I think you should call 911. Tell them what happened."

Kennedy hadn't expected that. The police? But then again, the idea made sense. Maybe they could trace the number. Maybe they could actually find the girl. Get her some real help.

Apparently, the matter was already certain in Carl's mind. "Tell them what you told me. And when you're done, call me back, just to let me know what they say."

Part of Kennedy wanted to ask Carl to do it. He was the director. But he hadn't talked with Rose. He couldn't give them the same details she could, details that might help the police stage a rescue. "All right," she agreed. "I'll call you back in a few."

"I'll be praying."

Kennedy's corneas were still dry and scratchy, as if somebody had blown cold air at her until each tear duct shriveled up like a parched, sandy desert. She disconnected her call with Carl and paused for a minute to calm down. Thoughts, prayers, blurred images clashed against one another discordantly in her mind. What had she gotten herself into? She was a high-achiever, but she knew when to admit she was in over her head. Nothing had equipped her for the past twenty minutes. That tiny, frightened voice kept replaying in her head until she couldn't think of anything else.

Kennedy was still staring at the hotline phone, as if Rose's last name and address might materialize on the screen if she got lucky enough. Then with a sigh, she dialed 911.

"The location of the emergency?" The operator's voice had an automatic, almost drone-like quality.

"It's not exactly an emergency. At least, I'm not sure it is."

"Your location?" he repeated, the smallest trace of annoyance creeping into his tone.

"I'm calling from Harvard."

"Square or University?"

"University. But that's not where the emergency is. I mean …" Kennedy tripped and stumbled over her words but finally described her conversation with Rose.

The dispatcher's tone didn't change. "So you're calling us because ...?"

"The director told me to," she answered. Why had it sounded like a good idea at the time? "He thought maybe you'd have a way to trace the call or something."

"Not without special equipment. And we can't trace calls after they're placed, anyway."

They were the police. They were supposed to protect innocent people, like thirteen-year-old girls who end up pregnant and terrified, talking to strangers when there's nobody else to turn to. "So there's nothing you can do?"

"No." She wondered if he spoke in a monotone all the time or only when he was on the clock. "And even if we could, there wouldn't be enough evidence for us to take action at this point."

Frustration and rage sandwiched Kennedy's arteries, and she felt her blood pressure escalate with her pulse. "What do you mean there's no evidence?" Had he been listening to her at all?

"She didn't accuse anybody, for one thing," the operator remarked. "In fact, there's not even proof at this point that she's pregnant at all. She could have just wanted some extra attention, create some false sympathy ..."

You didn't hear her voice, Kennedy wanted to scream.

Why had she thought the police would be able to do anything? The dispatcher didn't believe Rose's story. Next thing, he'd start telling Kennedy *she* was the one making things up and looking for extra attention.

"So you're basically saying I'm wasting my time trying to figure out how to help her. Is that it?" Kennedy heard the sharp edge in her own voice but didn't try to soften it.

"Without more information, there's nothing we can do."

"She said she was homeschooled," Kennedy suddenly remembered. "Can't you guys run a list or something of the families around here that homeschool their kids? See if there's a girl named Rose?"

"And then what?"

Kennedy thought she picked up a hint of sarcasm although the operator's tone didn't change from its irritating, robotic lull.

She didn't answer. So there really wasn't anything they could do? Not even trace a simple call. How hard could it really be? They did it all the time in movies, right? "What if she calls back?" Kennedy asked. "Could you trace a call then?"

The operator let out a sound that was a mix between a chuckle and a sigh. "Theoretically, maybe. But we'd need a lot more evidence before we'd set something like that up."

The last ounces of hope deflated out of Kennedy's lungs. "So there's nothing we can do."

"Well, if she calls back, you can always try to get a last name. See if you can figure out if she really is being abused or not."

Maybe the girl would call back. She could always hope. "But what if she doesn't give me her name?"

"Encourage her to call 911. Or talk to someone, a teacher or something."

"She's homeschooled," Kennedy reminded him, but the operator didn't respond. "All right," she finally sighed. "I guess that's all."

"Sorry we couldn't be more help." The words came automatically, and Kennedy doubted he meant them.

"Ok." She hung up and stared at the phone. Her first 911 call, and he had basically told her he couldn't lift a pinky finger to help. Exhaustion clung to her limbs as she made her way up the stairs to her dorm room. She'd have to call Carl back and tell him there was nothing to be done.

All right, God, she prayed. *You heard him. If you want me to help, Rose is going to have to call back.*

CHAPTER 4

Kennedy spent some time that evening looking up abortion methods online. The information she found both sickened and saddened her. Her initial search brought up several sites aimed specifically at young girls like Rose. *You don't need to feel guilty for choosing to end an unwanted pregnancy. Many girls have this procedure. It is quick, easy, and much safer than childbirth.*

As Kennedy read on, she couldn't stop thinking about those pictures in her dad's pro-life magazine showing what an aborted baby looks like. She jumped a little when her roommate threw open the door and swept into the room. Kennedy closed her browser. She had to get to work on some real studying, anyway.

"I thought you'd be out tonight," Kennedy remarked. In the past two months since they first came to Harvard, Willow hadn't spent a single night in on the weekend.

"I'm not staying." Willow sprayed some mousse into her

hands and scrunched it through her hair. "I'm just waiting for Keegan."

"Who's Keegan?" At first, Kennedy had tried to keep track of Willow's dates, but when she realized her roommate hardly saw anyone more than once or twice, she gave up the habit.

"Keegan. I thought I told you about him. He's Cesario in *Twelfth Night*."

Kennedy watched Willow crumple her hair into gravity-defying curls and waves. "Isn't Cesario supposed to be played by a girl?"

Willow shrugged and studied herself in her little desk mirror. "This version is sort of a modern retelling. Drag queens, bisexuals ... Shakespeare would've loved it."

Kennedy watched Willow put on some colorful bead earrings she had made herself and wondered how her roommate found time for crafts.

Willow glanced over at Kennedy's computer. "What are you studying?"

"Oh, I just got a lab I need to get ready to turn in on Monday."

Willow, who could hardly ever sit still for more than five seconds, crossed her arms and eyed Kennedy critically. "You ok?"

Kennedy didn't think she had done such a bad job hiding her stress about Rose's phone call. She definitely didn't want to talk about it with Willow, who probably believed Carl and Sandy's pregnancy center would set back women's rights by half a century or more. "I'm fine. Just tired."

Her roommate frowned. "You don't need to talk or anything?"

What was this? Willow sounded like Kennedy's mother, who always had an uncanny way of knowing if something was bothering her. "I'm fine. I really am."

Willow raised her eyes to the ceiling as if she were trying to remember the lines for a play. Finally she lowered them to give Kennedy a penetrating stare. "I'm just asking because I saw you on an abortion site. Are you in trouble?"

Kennedy let out a nervous laugh. No wonder Willow had been so concerned. It was sort of endearing, but also a little troubling. Didn't Willow know her well enough by now to understand Kennedy's values? "I wasn't looking it up for me."

Her roommate frowned. "It's nothing to be ashamed of. You wouldn't be the first Christian girl to get knocked up on campus."

"It's really not for me." Kennedy didn't have the energy to tell Willow everything about Rose and the hotline phone.

She hoped her roommate's date, Keegan, or whatever his name was, would show up soon.

Willow shrugged. "All right. Just remember, the longer you wait to deal with it, the harder it is. They even have pills now. So much easier than sitting in stirrups with a doctor and nurse gaping down at you."

Kennedy wanted to shut her ears.

"The thing with the pills is you can only take them in the first few weeks. So if you are in trouble, now's the time to do something about it. I know a good clinic I could recommend. You know me. I'm the last person to judge." Willow had stopped staring at Kennedy and was now pouting in the mirror as she applied her eye makeup. "I mean, I know you're probably all pro-life and everything, but there are obviously going to be exceptions, like when the mother's safety is threatened."

Kennedy didn't say anything. The more she insisted the research was for someone else, the more Willow would doubt her, anyway.

Willow adjusted her earrings. "Whatever you do, don't become a martyr like that Morphia lady or whatever her name was. You know who I'm talking about?"

Kennedy shook her head.

"Right, I keep forgetting you spent your teenage years

overseas on some mission of mercy with your parents or something. It was huge news around here last year. Some lady denying chemotherapy since she thought it would harm her baby. Made huge headlines. Of course, the anti-abortionists had a heyday about it. When she died, you would have thought she was a war hero on the crusade to abolish the murder of little fetuses or something. Anyway, the way I see it, if she didn't want her kid getting radiation from chemo, she should have been on the pill."

Kennedy started to say something in reply, but Willow wasn't done with her monologue.

"And don't get me started when you're talking about little kids. Can you believe there are actually politicians who say that if a girl is raped by her dad, she should still be expected to carry the baby to term? I mean, even someone as conservative as you could see how ridiculous that is to make a twelve- or thirteen-year-old actually go through nine months of pregnancy and all the risks of childbirth. They'd actually rather see the girl die than take care of it right at the beginning when it's safe."

Kennedy didn't answer. The mention of thirteen-year-olds and their fathers made her full stomach spin in protest. She didn't agree with Willow. She knew abortion was wrong regardless of the circumstances. But why? She hadn't thought through it thoroughly enough to be able to enter into any sort of debate.

Willow shrugged. Her phone buzzed once and she sprang out of her seat. "That'll be Keegan. Gotta go." She flashed Kennedy the same smile that made her perfect for stage acting. "Don't wait up for me." She flounced out of the room, leaving the door open a crack behind her.

Kennedy sighed and reached down into her book bag. She had work to do, and Monday would be here before she was ready.

CHAPTER 5

Kennedy was used to being surrounded by people. The past decade in Yanji gave her quite a different definition of *crowded* than most other Americans. Still, her pulse sped up when she entered St. Margaret's Church for Sunday services. For the past ten years, church had taken place in her parents' den and consisted of her, her mom and dad, and the few North Korean refugees that lived with them.

A woman in a denim skirt welcomed her at the door, and Kennedy didn't know if she was supposed to shake the outstretched hand or just accept the bulletin it offered. "Are you a visitor here?" the greeter asked, and Kennedy wondered in a church this size how someone could possibly keep track of who was new and who wasn't. Was there some kind of glossy look in Kennedy's eyes that gave it away? She explained that the Lindgrens were old family friends and entered the main sanctuary.

In Yanji, Kennedy's Korean housemates would often

arrive in the den thirty or forty minutes before services officially started. They kept the lights off and kneeled in darkness, offering a chorus of praise all at the same time. Tears, sobs, prayers, and petitions from each individual rose up to heaven simultaneously. At the time, Kennedy had found the noise chaotic and a tad frightening, but it was nothing like the din at St. Margaret's. The noise created an almost physical barrier that Kennedy struggled to pass through on her way to the pews. Children ran around haphazardly, shouting, waving, bumping into the legs of unsuspecting congregants. A whole gaggle of teen girls giggled loudly in a huddle. A mother of three snapped at her oldest to hold onto his little sister's hand. Behind her, two men bantered good-naturedly about the upcoming football game.

There was a band on the stage, with three guitars, a gleaming drum set, a keyboard, and a saxophone. Kennedy suspected there must be some sort of method in the musicians' warm-up, but it sounded like each one was vying to create the loudest, most obnoxious sound. Back in Yanji, Kennedy and the others had sung plenty of hymns, but there wasn't even a piano for accompaniment. She shut her eyes for a moment, trying to will away the noise, trying to recall the sounds of worship in her parents' den. During the ten years she spent in China, Kennedy always felt like the outsider. Now, in the second-to-back pew in the crowded auditorium, she realized she'd give about anything for a day or two back home.

The band played its first harmonious bar, and the talking and bedlam reluctantly died down as people took their seats. The ensuing music, however, was even louder than the hundreds of tiny conversations that had stopped. Kennedy clenched shut her eyes, wishing for some sort of cocoon to shield her from the volume. Was this how Americans worshipped every single Sunday?

She didn't recognize the song, and it wasn't until the tall gentleman in front of her shifted slightly to make room for his wife that Kennedy realized the words were being projected onto the wall above the stage. She glanced around, more self-conscious and out-of-place than she ever had felt on foreign soil, even though she had no logical reason to worry about her image. Nobody was paying any attention to her. The man a few seats over was busy scrolling on his phone. The woman in front of him was texting. Behind Kennedy, a preschooler kicked the back of her seat in a near approximation to the music's beat. A woman in the aisle over was having a full conversation with the mother behind her, and here and there some of the attendees raised their hands in worship.

Kennedy had never considered her house-church experience as novel or foreign or even very interesting, at least not until now. Back in Yanji, she could have isolated the voice of each individual singer. Hannah had a high, ringing soprano. Her friend Simon couldn't carry a tune to save his life, but what he lacked in musical talent he made up for in sheer loudness. Levi probably could have gone on to become a South Korean pop sensation or something if he hadn't returned to North Korea as an undercover missionary. Where were they all now? And how meaningful would it be if Kennedy had a chance to worship together with them again?

The song itself was poignant, something that probably could have grabbed her attention if she heard it on the radio. The lyrics spoke of longing, yearning. *My heart is homesick for your glory, Lord.* At that line, her throat constricted and she stopped mouthing the words. *Homesick.* She didn't know when she'd go back to Yanji. Maybe over Christmas break, maybe not until next summer. Even then, would it ever be the same?

Kennedy wrapped her arms across her chest. She wanted to hide. She wanted to run away, forget about pining for another place, forget about the homesickness that threatened to hack her heart to pieces. If she left now, would anyone around her notice? Would they care? Or were they too busy texting or worshipping to pay any attention?

The song ended, followed by another almost exactly like it. Had there really been a time when Kennedy thought the hymns they sang back in Yanji were boring and dry? Toward the front of the sanctuary, a young man with blond dreadlocks lifted both hands high over his head. His eyes were closed in rapture. Jealousy slithered its way up and around Kennedy's shoulders. Could she ever worship God that openly, that freely? She had watched the North Koreans in her parents' home sing praises with tears flowing down their cheeks, but she had never experienced anything remotely similar. Her father said that everyone relates to God in his or her own unique way, but Kennedy sometimes wondered if she really related to God at all. Or had God become such an everyday part of her life that there was no room left for awe?

After a few more songs, Pastor Carl climbed the steps to the stage. Just the sight of his face was a comfort in this rippling sea of strangers. His voice was soothing, something familiar. He gave some brief updates about small groups and then announced the opening of the new pregnancy center. When the cheers died down, he invited everyone to Thursday night's kick-off dinner. "Right here at St. Margaret's. Our special guest speaker will be State Senator Wayne Abernathy, who I've asked to come up and say the morning's blessing."

A tall, hair-sprayed man with the smile of a TV newscaster stood up to an even peppier round of applause and made his way to the platform. He shook Pastor Carl's hand, beaming the whole time, and waved to the audience with his free arm.

"Wayne is Massachusetts' most dedicated pro-life advocate," Carl declared. "He's been toiling tirelessly for the cause of the unborn child for the past eight years in the State House, and as most of you know, he's now running for governor." More applause. "Brother," Carl continued, "we'd like to thank you for being one of the pro-life movement's most devoted front-lines warriors, and we wish you God's blessings in the election next week and in all your future endeavors. Would you be so kind as to pray and bless this morning's service?"

Kennedy shut her eyes automatically when the prayer started but flung them open again at the sound of a muffled *Brahms' Lullaby.* She snatched her book bag, scurried to her feet, and tried to weave past the legs of those sitting next to her. The ringtone was starting its second refrain when she scampered out the massive double doors of the sanctuary.

"Hello?" She was so breathless that she didn't bother trying to get the name of the pregnancy center right this time.

"It's me."

Kennedy kept her breath trapped inside for fear she might blow away the quiet voice. "Rose? Are you ok?" Some teens and a few adults were loitering in the foyer, and Kennedy glanced around for someplace private.

"My uncle heard us talking."

Kennedy froze. "So he knows?" The sensation reminded her of a free-fall ride at a carnival.

"Yeah."

In one ear, Kennedy could still hear the politician's prayer from the main stage. She hurried down the hall, hoping to find a library or small study where they could talk in peace. "How did he react?"

"Says I need to get rid of it."

"The baby, you mean?" Kennedy tried a doorknob and found a tiny storage room. It definitely wasn't the coziest spot in the church, but at least she was alone.

Rose didn't respond.

"What do you want?" Kennedy prompted. "Do you want to get rid of the baby, too?"

"No." Her voice was even smaller.

"Well, nobody can make you." Kennedy hoped that was

true. She didn't really know what would happen if the mother was a minor. Could her parents force an abortion on her? Kennedy needed to talk to Carl, but that couldn't happen until after his sermon.

"He already made the appointment," the girl whispered.

"Do you know when that will be? Or what clinic he's taking you to?" What was Kennedy planning? To show up and whisk Rose away before the abortion started?

"He just told me he'd take care of it."

Kennedy thought about Amy Carmichael, the missionary who literally stole girls away from temple slavery. As a child listening to the tales, Kennedy hadn't thought twice about going to such extreme lengths to save somebody. After all, her own parents sheltered North Korean refugees right under the nose of the Chinese government. But this was different. This was the United States, the alleged home of the free.

"Is there somewhere we could meet?" Kennedy asked. "I have some friends, the ones who run the pregnancy center. I know they'd find a way to help you."

Something beeped in Kennedy's ear. She looked at the phone. *You've got to be kidding.* The battery light was blinking. Carl hadn't even given her a charger. Then she noticed the number actually showed up this time on the screen. She could call Rose back. They might be able to locate her.

It was all Kennedy could do to keep her voice down as she rummaged through her book bag for her personal cell. "Listen, this phone is about to die. But I want to keep on talking to you." Where was it? Had she left it in her dorm room? She hurried out of the closet. There had to be a landline phone somewhere. "If we get disconnected, I want you to just wait. Wait there by the phone, and I'll call you right back. Ok?"

"You can't do that." It was probably the most forceful thing Rose had said, but even so her voice never grew above a hush.

"It's all right." Relief warmed Kennedy's face when she saw an open office door, and she hurried in. "I'm here to help you, remember. So if we get connected, I'm going to ..."

"Don't," the girl whispered, and then the line went dead.

Not yet. Kennedy wanted to throw the phone against the wall. Why couldn't the batteries have lasted a few more seconds? Now she wouldn't be able to bring the number up ...

Wait a minute. The battery light blinked faintly. There was still a little bit of power left. Rose must have hung up. But why? It didn't matter. Kennedy wasn't going to miss this opportunity. She checked the caller ID, settled down in the office chair, and punched the number into the desk phone with a resolute hand.

Busy.

She hung up and redialed.

Still busy.

Had Rose taken the phone off the hook, then? Was she scared of Kennedy calling?

"Can I help you?"

Kennedy jumped at the sound, and her faced reddened. It was the man with dreadlocks. He was wearing khaki shorts and a T-shirt with a picture of Jesus surfing in bare feet without any board. Kennedy guessed he had found himself on the wrong coast. New Englanders didn't dress that way. Especially not for church.

"Is everything all right?" Two stray dreads swung in his face when he cocked his head to the side.

"I'm sorry," Kennedy stammered. "Is this ... I needed to make an emergency phone call, and the door was open, so I ... Is this your desk?" She looked down and saw a picture of Mr. Dreads with his arm around a bronze, blond-haired Barbie girl. Even though her two-piece swimsuit only showed an inch or so of her belly, Kennedy immediately noted the hint of her six-pack. "I'm sorry," Kennedy repeated.

The man held up his hand. "It's no problem." He glanced

at the phone. "Did you get hold of whoever you were looking for?"

"No. I ... I actually really need to talk to Carl. But I guess he's busy right now, isn't he?"

He laughed. "Well, the good news is it's a football Sunday. Which means he won't preach a minute past twelve twenty-five."

Kennedy couldn't immediately grasp how that could be considered good news. "Do you mind if I try your phone just one more time?"

He shrugged. "Have at it."

Busy again.

"Dang it."

She hadn't meant to say that out loud. She glanced at the clock. Thirty minutes until the sermon ended. She imagined Rose's uncle dragging her to his car and forcing her into an abortion clinic before Carl made it to his closing prayer.

"Is it something I can help with? I'm Nick, by the way. I'm the youth and children's pastor here." He gave a little wave but didn't offer his hand. "I actually just came down the hall because I left my Bible, but hey, if you're in trouble or something ..."

"I really need to talk to Carl."

Nick glanced at her out of the corner of his eye, and

Kennedy wondered if he was trying to gauge her sanity.

"I'm one of the volunteers at the new pregnancy center," she decided to explain. "I've been getting these calls on the hotline phone ..."

A moment later, Nick was perched up on the corner of his desk, nodding empathetically. Kennedy was too emotionally drained to relive each individual detail, but she spewed out the basic premise of her two calls from Rose.

"So I tried to call her back," she concluded, "but I kept getting a busy signal."

"Well, at least you have a number now, right? I mean, now you can find out where she's calling from, get the police involved if you're really concerned."

Kennedy wasn't sure the police would be any more willing to help this time than they had been the other evening, but it was a step in the right direction. At least now, she could keep trying to re-establish communication. And if she needed to, she could probably use the phone number to get a last name or a location or something.

"Here." Nick leaned down and swiveled the screen of his computer around. He reached over for the keyboard and placed it on his lap.

"Are you sure I'm not taking up all your time? I mean, you're probably really busy on Sundays."

"Nah." Nick waved his hand in the air. "Don't tell anyone, but Pastor Carl's sermons usually put me to sleep."

Kennedy wasn't sure she believed him, but she didn't argue. She was grateful to find someone who was taking the hotline call seriously.

"Here we go." Nick had typed in a web address for a reverse phone number site. "Tell me the number, and we'll see what we get."

She read him the digits. He stopped typing halfway through.

"Read that again." His eyes narrowed, and he gave Kennedy a suspicious sideways look.

She repeated it.

He reached out his hand. "Let me see that."

She handed him the phone and watched his tanned face pale a little. Foreboding sank down in her stomach like a rock and settled there. "What's wrong?"

Nick didn't take his eyes off the cell. "This is the number for St. Margaret's. Whoever she is, she was calling from inside the church."

CHAPTER 6

"This better not be one of your silly tricks to keep me away from my football game."

Kennedy heard Carl's good-natured voice reverberate through the halls a few seconds before he entered Nick's office.

"Kennedy! So you did come!" He spread his arms out for a hug and then stopped. "Something happened." He looked to Nick. "Is this the big problem that couldn't wait?" He frowned even though his voice hadn't lost its kindly tone.

Nick nodded. "She says that …"

"The girl call back again?" Carl interrupted.

Once they found a way to help Rose, Kennedy figured she could go a whole year without talking about the past few days and that still wouldn't be long enough. "She said her uncle found out, listened in to our last call or something. Said he's already scheduled her an abortion." She handed Carl the phone, half hoping to hear *Brahms' Lullaby*, half hoping to never see it again.

Wrinkles materialized on Carl's face the same way splotches popped up on Kennedy's skin when she got nervous.

"Wait until you hear the weirdest part," Nick said.

Kennedy took a deep breath. "She didn't call from a blocked number this time. We checked the ID. She was calling from here."

A heavy silence billowed up like a cloud of gas over a lab beaker. Carl heaved a massive sigh. "How long ago was that call?"

"About half an hour." Kennedy had been staring at the clock, counting down the seconds since Rose hung up.

"Think she's still here?"

Nick shrugged. "She could be anywhere."

"There's nobody named Rose in youth group, is there?" Carl asked.

Nick shook his head.

"But she might have made up a name," Carl mused. He made Kennedy describe both phone calls in as much detail as she could muster up. Maybe Nick could recognize Rose. After a sophisticated version of the guessing game, minus the good humor and laughter, they still hadn't made any progress.

"Did you find out anything else about her family?" Carl

asked. "Something that might make them stick out from anyone else in the church?"

"She mentioned her uncle, and she mentioned her dad. That's all." Kennedy's stomach was churning.

"No brothers or sisters?" Nick prompted.

Kennedy's contacts were scratching at her eyes again. "I told you everything she told me," she huffed.

Carl stood up. "Well, you've certainly gone above and beyond the call of duty." He placed a strong hand on her shoulder. The gesture reminded her of her father, and she wished she could shut her eyes and click her heels together and end up back in Yanji. She could postpone college for a year, or maybe take classes online.

"Well, how about I'll drop you back off at school. Nick and I will keep thinking. We'll find a way to check who was in the junior high Sunday school today, things like that."

"It'll be a lot easier finding her now that we know what church she goes to," Nick added.

"But I do want to be discreet about it all," Carl muttered to Nick, "what with the timing and everything."

"Of course."

Carl gave Kennedy's shoulder an encouraging squeeze. "Cheer up. Let me drive you back to campus."

They slipped out of the office. "I got my car parked

around the corner." Carl beeped the button on his automatic keys.

"What about Sandy?" Kennedy asked. "I didn't see her all morning."

"She left right after the service ended. Went to drop off a few things at the center, do a little planning for the dinner."

Kennedy slipped into the passenger seat of Carl's maroon Honda. He groaned as he plopped down next to her. "I'm getting too old for this," he mumbled. "Now where are those keys? I just had them."

She smiled to herself while she watched him turn his pockets inside out one by one, but all she really wanted to do was get back to her dorm and grab some lunch. She had to meet Reuben in an hour to finish going over their lab report. If they started right away, she might finish in time to get a decent chunk of her Russian lit reading done before crashing for the night. In addition to her calculus test, she had papers due in both her literature classes next week. When Carl's air conditioning blew in her face, she blinked her eyes and made a mental note to call her dad tonight about those contacts.

Carl finally found his keys under his leg as a phone beeped. Kennedy automatically opened her backpack before she remembered her cell wasn't there. "That's not me," she told Carl. "Did someone just text you?"

He fumbled for another minute before pulling out his thick cell phone. He squinted over his glasses. "Uh-oh." He was already dialing before Kennedy could ask what was wrong.

"Hi, babe. Are you ok?" He swung the car backwards out into a wide arch as he pulled out of his parking spot. Kennedy looked back over her shoulder to make sure they weren't about to ram into anything. Her shoulder slammed the passenger door when he straightened out and pumped the gas. "Sorry," he whispered to her.

Kennedy checked to make sure her seat belt was tight.

"No, no, no. I'm coming over right now." Carl was almost yelling. "Well if it's too dangerous for me, then I'm not about to just leave you there ... You're sure you're not hurt? ... Ok, we're already on our way ... Yeah, I've got Kennedy here with me. Stay put. And stay away from the windows, all right? Go in the back office and lock the door until I get there ... Fine, stay until the police get there then ... Be safe, baby. I love you."

His complexion had paled several degrees by the time he hung up. "Sandy's run into some problems at the pregnancy center. We need to stop and make sure everything's all right."

Kennedy saw the way the vein in his neck twitched and

didn't ask for any more information. His knuckles were almost white against the steering wheel. She sensed it wasn't the appropriate time to joke about him missing his afternoon football game.

Carl sped the entire time and broke several other traffic laws as he weaved his way through the lazy weekend traffic. When he finally turned onto Elm Street, the whole sidewalk was littered with people. Some waved picket signs. Others shouted. Kennedy couldn't distinguish the words but felt the vibrations of their angry yells like a low, violent rumble. Down the road a ways were two parked police cars, their red and blue siren lights spinning in the midday sun.

Carl snaked his way into a parallel parking spot next to some yellow police tape. "Stay here." He slammed the door shut behind him and jostled his way down the sidewalk with fists clenched. Kennedy jumped out and followed him.

"What's going on?" he demanded as a policewoman walked up.

"Sir, this is a zoned area. Please stay behind the tape."

"My wife is in that building." Carl had to yell to be heard. Kennedy didn't notice until then the broken glass glistening on the pavement. Two other police officers were holding back crowds while picketers waved around signs with sayings like, *Keep Your Regulations Off My Uterus*, and *Pro-Choice or No Choice*. Kennedy stayed close by Carl's shoulder.

"Your wife's in there, you say?" the police officer repeated.

"She just called me a few minutes ago."

A young man hollered, "Hey, aren't you the pastor at that mega-church?"

Carl glared but said nothing.

The guy waved his hand in the air and pointed. "This is the pastor. The one who opened up the clinic."

A few people started shouting, and even though nobody made their way closer to the yellow tape, the policewoman grabbed Carl by the elbow. "Come on. Let's get you inside."

Kennedy stepped as gingerly as she could around the broken glass while trying to keep up with them. "Sandy!" Carl shouted as soon as they got into the center, but all Kennedy noticed were the walls splashed with crass pictures, angry slogans, and an obscene statement or two. It felt as if someone hit her in the gut and then left his fist there to fester.

"Sandy!" Carl repeated.

"I'll be back to ask you some questions later." Kennedy doubted Carl heard the police officer before she went out the front door.

"Oh, thank God they let you through!" At the sound of Sandy's voice, Kennedy pried her eyes away from the grotesque graffiti. Sandy rushed to Carl, the extra fabric of her floral dress fluttering around her ankles, and they embraced. Kennedy thought she saw Carl's broad shoulders tremble, but when they pulled apart, his voice was clear and resolute.

"Baby, tell me exactly what happened."

"I came straight from church. The protestors were already here, at least some of them. At first, I didn't even notice the broken windows. I thought they were just doing their picketing thing. You know, they've got as much a right to these sidewalks as the rest of us. I was going to walk my way in here and not let them bother me. Well, by the time I was out of the car, that's when I saw the glass. And some guy starts following me real close, asking me what I'm doing around the center, making rude comments. Then another woman, one of the protestors, started shouting at him, telling him he shouldn't intimidate me no matter who I am. Then she asks me what I'm doing here, and I tell her my husband and I opened this clinic, and she apologizes for the broken glass. Says it was like that when she got here, and if she had seen who did it she would have reported it to the police. Then she asks if I want to go in, and she just marches up with me, and tells me that we're women and we have to ..." Sandy's voice caught, and Kennedy stared at her shoes while Sandy continued. "Says we have to stick together, no matter if we have our political differences. And once she sees me safe in here, she tells me again she's sorry for the mess. And then she takes her *Hands Off My Uterus* sign and goes back out with the rest of them."

Carl and Kennedy were both quiet. Carl was running his hand through his wife's light brown hair, but Kennedy couldn't take her eyes off the walls.

"I just can't believe how insensitive people can be." Sandy shook her head. "They've got their right to picket. They've got their right to be heard. But they don't care about our rights, and now look at this mess."

Kennedy had been trying to figure out a particular image spray-painted on the wall. "What's up with the hanger? What does that have to do with ...?" It felt like someone grabbed the inside of her stomach and twisted a full three-hundred-sixty degrees. "Oh."

"There's more." Sandy glanced over at her husband. "You want to see the worst now or later?"

"May as well get it over with." Carl followed Sandy to the back office. She was a tall woman but looked half a foot shorter by the time they arrived there.

Kennedy's nervous chuckle sounded out of place as it echoed against the walls. "What's so intimidating about a cookie?"

"I'm sorry, babe," Sandy whispered.

Kennedy glanced at Carl.

"Oreo," he explained in a lifeless monotone. "Black on the outside. White on the inside."

Sandy shut the door and pointed at the wall. "If it makes you feel any better, I got my own message, too." The room suddenly felt twice as small. Sandy had moved the wall calendar to cover some of the letters, but Kennedy could still see the huge red *N* and the bottom half of the word *lover* underneath.

Carl and Sandy held each other for several minutes in silence. Kennedy didn't know where to look or what to say. Indignation welled up in her chest like pressure building up in a sealed flask. These were her friends. From her earliest memories, the Lindgrens had been helping people, loving people, taking people into their homes. They didn't deserve any of this. She wondered what her dad would say. Would he have the words to make sense of this type of hatred and emotional violence? Kennedy wrapped her arms around herself again, but that did nothing to stop her trembling.

"Father God ..." Carl's words were loud and sounded completely out of place in the face of such darkness and shame. "I thank you for protecting my Sandy when she was here alone. And I thank you for the kind lady who helped her reach the center safely. And even though it tears me up inside God, I thank you for the jerk who insulted my wife on the sidewalk. I thank you for the stupid, blind, ignoramuses who desecrated our new center. Because somehow, I know you have a plan for them. And somehow, I know you love them. And if I have to be totally honest with you, Father, I have to admit that I would be just as lost and just as angry and just as hateful if you hadn't poured out your grace on me. So forgive me, Lord. Forgive me for the anger I feel. Forgive me for hating them for hurting my wife, making her feel unsafe."

Carl's voice caught, and Kennedy glanced up to see the tears splashing down his cheeks onto his wife's arms as they leaned their foreheads against each other.

"Forgive me, Lord, because I can't love these idiots like you do." Carl was crying softly now. Kennedy bit her lip, but that did nothing to contain her emotion.

"Lord, you're the King. You reign bigger than all this. You reign bigger than this center. You reign bigger than politics. You reign bigger than abortion or racism or intolerance or injustice. You reign bigger than the ignorance that has kept this country in darkness for so long. And now we're asking you to come into our little, humble, violated center today and show yourself bigger. Bigger than fear. Bigger than revenge. Bigger than any of their slurs or any of their hate speech or any of their rage. And be bigger than us, too. Bigger than our unforgiveness. Bigger than our hurt. Because, Father, you know we're hurting something awful right now."

There was no *amen*. Only a small, almost indistinguishable rushing in Kennedy's spirit. She opened her eyes. Carl and Sandy had already pulled apart and were laughing quietly at each other's tear-stained faces. Kennedy wasn't exactly sure what had just happened, but she recalled how insecure she had felt at St. Margaret's earlier. She thought about how small she had felt living with Secret Seminary students who risked North Korean death camps for the sake of the gospel. She thought about how envious she had felt when everyone around her was getting touched by God and she was left sitting in the bleachers to watch.

So maybe she hadn't lifted her hands in complete and utter abandon. Maybe she hadn't sung out her heart in ecstasy or faced a North Korean prison cell for her bold faith. But she had witnessed something more real than anything she had experienced since she returned to the States. She couldn't put a name to it and probably never could, but Kennedy knew she was somehow better for it, and she knew it was something she would carry in a sacred part of her heart for the rest of her life.

CHAPTER 7

Sandy made a list of paints to pick up from the store. Kennedy found a broom to sweep up the glass, but Carl didn't want her by the broken windows. "If you want to help, we still need to get these postcards ready to mail out. They're the invitations for the dinner on Thursday." He showed her how the post office needed them grouped by zip code, and Kennedy set to work, grateful for something constructive to put her hands to. She would be late meeting Reuben at the library, but she wasn't about to leave Carl and Sandy now.

"Is everyone all right back here?" The voice was too good-humored, and Kennedy looked up to see the politician who had prayed at the service that morning.

"Wayne!" Sandy rushed to him with a hug. Carl stretched out his hand.

"I came as soon as I heard the report on the Christian radio." Wayne shook his head. "It's just horrible what they've done."

"Nothing a little paint and some new glass won't fix." Carl's voice was still tight.

"How in the world did you get through the picket lines?" Sandy asked.

"Well, I think I made a record. I was only asked for three autographs." Wayne flashed another dizzying grin.

"Autographs?" Carl asked. He leaned out of the office and let out a low whistle. "Well, what do you make of that? You had it easy, brother. Those weren't the picketers we had to walk through. It was all pro-choicers when we came."

"They're on the other side of the sidewalk now," Wayne told them. He locked eyes with Sandy. "You really should go take a look."

Kennedy followed Carl and Sandy into the waiting room. The police tape was gone. Half a dozen police lined either side of the road. All the protestors from earlier were on the opposite sidewalk, but those closest to the broken window had pickets with statistics about fetal development, Bible verses about God knitting children together in the womb, and slogans about protecting babies.

"That's quite a different view than when we arrived earlier," Carl admitted.

"I'll say." Wayne flashed a grin.

"You and your campaign didn't have anything to do with

this new turn of events, did they?" Sandy asked with a smile in her voice.

Wayne flashed his white-toothed grin. "I don't speak for my managers. All I know is these picketers were here when I pulled up."

"Uh-huh." Sandy's voice was playful, and she smiled for the first time that afternoon.

Wayne smoothed out his hair and straightened his necktie. "Anyway, we're making a statement from here for the press in about half an hour."

"From here?" Sandy repeated. "They can't bring the cameras into this mess." Her eyes fluttered nervously to the walls.

Wayne frowned at the graffiti. "I guess we can do it up front by the window. I told my manager we should work in a little announcement about the fundraising dinner Thursday. Couldn't hurt to get you guys some more publicity."

"Unless the picketers scare off all the donors," Sandy mumbled under her breath, but Kennedy doubted the others heard.

"Well, then." Wayne clasped his hands together. "That's settled. What do we do while we wait for the cameramen?"

Carl caught Kennedy's eye and gave her a wink. "How would the soon-to-be governor of Massachusetts feel about stamping postcards?"

The mood in the center lifted minute by minute as they set to work. Once Kennedy finished the pile she was sorting, she figured it was time to head back to campus. If she got lucky and caught the T as it was pulling up, she might find Reuben still in the library. Before she could slip out, Wayne's phone rang.

He slipped his hand smoothly into his pocket. "I bet that's about the statement." The conversation was short. "They're ready for me out front." Wayne was beaming, and Kennedy wondered if Carl and Sandy noticed how fake he looked. Maybe it was a politician thing. Or maybe all the support and publicity he brought to their center helped them overlook his apparent insincerity. Whatever it was, Kennedy was glad for an excuse to leave before she had to watch him preen in front of a dozen cameras.

"I need to go, too." she announced. Sandy cast a worried glance to her husband.

"Maybe you better wait," Carl said. "After Wayne's speech, I'll drive you back myself. Your father would kill me if I let you walk out of here with hundreds of angry protestors looking on."

"I'm sure it will be fine," Kennedy insisted, but she looked at the Lindgrens' expressions and didn't want to burden them further. "I'm supposed to meet my friend," she explained, "but I guess a few more minutes won't kill anyone."

"Do you want to use the phone to let her know you're late?" Sandy asked.

"I don't have his number with me. It's in my phone, and that's somewhere in my dorm room."

"*His?*" Carl asked but stopped smirking when his wife nudged him in the ribs.

"Carl will drive you back as soon as Wayne's done posing for the cameras." Sandy gave Kennedy a gentle back rub. "And don't worry — he won't take more than a few minutes I'm sure. The last thing he wants to do is bore his audience."

Carl chuckled under his breath. Sandy was right. The speech was over in less than five minutes. Kennedy had expected the Lindgrens to both stop their work to listen, but they seemed content to keep on sorting postcards side by side.

"Did you wow them?" Sandy asked when Wayne pranced back into the center to a loud roar of both applause and angry shouts. He looked even taller than he had before he left.

"All I have to say is I hope something I said got through to the fools who vandalized your center." He shook his head, replacing his smile for an instant pout that became him just as well.

Sandy patted his shoulder. "Well, you keep focused on

winning your election and don't worry about us. We've seen worse, you know."

Kennedy wasn't sure if she had seen worse or not and was sad to think that Carl and Sandy had.

"You heading out now?" Carl asked when Wayne started to button up his coat.

"Sure am. I wish I could stay to help more, but ..." He stumbled over his words for the first time, but neither of the Lindgrens seemed to notice.

Sandy put down her pile of invites and gave him a hug. "It's always good to see you. Thanks for taking time out of your campaign to check on us commoners." Everyone chuckled, and Kennedy was left guessing if Sandy meant to be sarcastic or not.

"Well, if you're heading out ..." Carl inserted, and Kennedy wished she could stop him with telepathy. "Would you mind taking Kennedy here back to her dorm at Harvard?"

"Harvard, huh?" Wayne's face brightened, and he spared Kennedy his first glance since showing up. "Sure thing. My car's out back."

Kennedy glanced at the Lindgrens, who were only a quarter of the way through the postcards they had to sort. Maybe it was just as well they both stayed here. Besides, she hadn't thought about it before, but now that Carl was marked as the director of the center, it might still be dangerous for him to walk out right now. Wayne was way too-high profile for someone to seriously bother. She said good-bye to Carl and Sandy and followed him out the center. The sound of the protestors increased, but Wayne put his arm around her, and whispered before she could shrug him off, "Don't listen to anything they say. Their words can't hurt you. All right?"

Kennedy nodded and tried to recreate the calm she had felt when Carl prayed in the center. Many of the pro-lifers extended their hands to Wayne, and others offered encouraging words about the election next week. He kept his arm around her like a shield as a photographer flashed a light at them and a reporter shoved a microphone in his face.

"Mr. Abernathy, is this one of the young women you would deny contraceptives and access to safe abortions?"

Wayne didn't slow down his pace but waved the microphone away.

They got to his car, which he circled once and studied with a frown. Looking for dents? Then he turned on his shiny smile and opened the passenger door. "After you," he stated regally.

The upholstery had that sort of new lacquer smell, and

when Kennedy sat down, she found it hard to get comfortable because her pants kept sticking to the seat. Even the seatbelt buckle glistened. Kennedy wondered how many semesters at Harvard Wayne's car would pay for.

"You ready?" he asked when he got into the driver's seat.

Kennedy smiled in response, and he rolled out of the lot. They hadn't passed the outlying protestors when his phone rang. "Hey. I'm on the road. What's up?"

Kennedy let out her breath when they finally turned off Elm Street. She wondered how all the other shop and business owners felt about having their sidewalks turned into an ideological war zone.

"Good news?" Wayne was apparently one of those people who shouted into their cell phones as if that was the only way to be heard. "Those were my friends whose office was attacked ... Well, it's your job to worry about publicity, not mine. I'm just glad nobody got hurt."

He shook his head as he hung up. "My campaign manager," he explained with a sigh. "Acts as though this protest is Christmas Day for the campaign. Sympathy votes and all." He gave Kennedy a smile, a real one this time, the corners of his eyes wrinkling up attractively. "So, what are you studying at Harvard? I just hope it's not politics."

"Biology."

His eyebrows shot up. "Oh yeah? Pre-med?"

"Sort of. I'm part of their early-admissions medical school program."

"Good for you." Kennedy was relieved to note Wayne could actually sound sincere if he wanted to. "You must have worked hard to get accepted right out of high school."

Kennedy didn't feel like talking about herself, so she asked, "What about you? When did you get involved with pro-life stuff?"

Wayne chuckled. "That would be a better question if I were driving you all the way to DC. The short version is I did picketing, things like that from Roe v. Wade on. I was part of the first wave of the anti-abortion movement, but I got frustrated. We got a little bit of publicity, made a lot of people angry, and preached to thousands of choirs. That was it. Don't quote me on this, but it was actually a staunch pro-abortion advocate who helped me see the light. You ever heard of Sandra Green?"

Kennedy shook her head.

Wayne shrugged. "Yeah, she hasn't been around in a while, at least not making news like years past. She used to be a real big voice for the abortion camp. But she was talking about a new bill we were hoping to push through the State House. I was just wetting my feet in politics at the time, you know. But she said something I'll never forget. Knocked me right off my high horse. Said that the reason nobody wants to jump on the pro-life bandwagon is because it's a bunch of stuffy old white men who have never lifted a finger to help single moms. And it was true. At least for me at the time. And a lot of my acquaintances. What was the point of stopping abortions if I wasn't going to help support new mothers? That's how I got my initiation into the pregnancy center ministry. Made it my mission to give women a foundation, maybe alleviate some of the perceived need for abortions in the first place."

Kennedy didn't know how to respond. She had never looked at abortion in those terms before. In her family, it was simply wrong, morally and ethically, and that was all.

"You from a Christian family?" Wayne asked after a minute. He had a disarming way of taking his eyes off the road to look at her when he talked.

"Yeah."

"Well, you just stick to your values. Especially on a campus like Harvard. It's not easy. Even more so now than when I was your age. But you keep following what your mom and dad taught you, and you're going to be fine." That plastic smile flashed again, and they spent the last few minutes traveling in silence. Kennedy got the impression Wayne wouldn't remember her face in a week, but she was thankful for the ride. He pulled his car into the main campus entrance. "Is this close enough?"

"Yeah," she answered. "This is just fine."

"Well, God bless you." He raised his hand in a wave, and for a minute she expected him to hand her a pen or a campaign button or something. As his car eased back into traffic, Kennedy wondered if Reuben would still be in the library. Her dorm was on the way, so she figured she'd grab her books and her cell phone. She needed something quick to eat, too. Her stomach had been churning and grumbling ever since St. Margaret's.

She felt light as she bounded up the stairs to her dorm, grateful her lab would give her an excuse to shove all thoughts of the pregnancy center and Rose out of her mind. The door to her room was halfway open, and Willow crossed her arms as soon as Kennedy entered.

"Your boyfriend's been looking for you."

CHAPTER 8

Kennedy knew if she took the time to sit down, she wouldn't get up again, but her bed tugged her toward it with an almost irresistible gravity. She threw her lab books into her backpack.

"So Reuben was here? Was he upset?"

Willow shrugged. "Does that guy ever get upset about anything? He must take, I don't know, ten Prozacs a day or something. Is he a weed head?"

Kennedy shook her head, only half listening. "I left my phone here this morning so I couldn't call him." She glanced around her desk and rummaged through her top drawer. "Hey, could you call me? I still can't find it."

Willow let out a long, dramatic sigh that could have won awards if she had actually been on the stage, but she punched the buttons on her phone. "It's ringing."

Kennedy spun herself around in a slow circle. "I don't hear it."

Willow turned her cell off. "Maybe you let your batteries go dead."

"Yeah, maybe." It certainly wouldn't have been the first time. The problem was she didn't have Reuben's number written down anywhere. She looked at her clock. Over an hour late. "He must think I'm such a flake. When did he stop by?"

Willow ran a hand through her long hair, which this week was tinted a somewhat convincing ginger tone. "Half hour ago, maybe? I don't know. I've been busy."

Kennedy glanced at the army shooter game on her roommate's computer. "Looks like it," she mumbled. "Hey, did he say where he was going to be? Did he mention the library?"

Willow was already back at her sniping. A fake death cry rang out as a puddle of red pixelated blood splashed on her screen. She didn't respond. Well, Kennedy would try to send him an email and then head to the library to see if he was still there.

Kennedy waited for her desktop to load and opened a granola bar. What had she had for breakfast? It seemed like so long ago. And she and Reuben had at least three or four hours of work ahead of them to finish up that report. All she really wanted to do was sleep off the stress of the day.

She glanced once more at her bed. Maybe a few minutes ...

Wonk. Wonk. Wonk.

Willow wrinkled her nose and covered her ears. "What's that noise?"

The resident advisor from the boys' side of the hall poked his head through their open door. "Fire drill," he called out.

Kennedy groaned. She didn't have time for this. She grabbed her backpack and decided to head right to the library. She could email Reuben from the computers there if she didn't find him. Willow was moaning about having to start her level over again as she and Kennedy plodded down the stairs along with the other sluggish students. Several dozen were already outside by the time they joined the throng.

"So there you are."

Kennedy turned toward the sound of Reuben's voice and tried to muster the energy to smile. "I'm sorry about our meeting. It's been a crazy day."

She didn't want to go into any details and was thankful when Reuben just remarked, "Hey, things come up. No big deal."

"Well, I would have called. But I didn't have my phone with me. I just got back to my dorm a few minutes ago, and

I still couldn't find it."

"No problem." Reuben's eyes twinkled, and Kennedy had to laugh at his endearing way of staying so composed. There wasn't much she suspected could make him mad, with the exception maybe of someone insulting one of his sisters.

"I was on my way to the library to look for you," she said. "Do you want to head there?"

"Sure." Reuben adjusted the straps of his backpack. "Did you print up the table from last week?"

Kennedy groaned. "I completely forgot. You know, things have been insane ever since that weird phone call Friday."

"Hey," Reuben insisted, "don't worry about it."

"We can go up now and grab it from my computer. Well, at least we can when this fire drill is over."

"So that's why you're all standing out here?" Reuben chuckled. "I thought somebody put something rotten in the vent and smoked you all out."

After a few minutes, the resident advisor shouted the all-clear, and Kennedy and Reuben headed up the stairs.

"Did your roommate tell you I stopped by?" he asked.

"Yeah. I'm sorry you had to come all the way over here for ..."

"You don't need to apologize any more. Your roommate's

very nice, by the way. Strange maybe, but nice."

Yeah, that's Willow. Kennedy kept the thought to herself. When they got to her room, she sat down and pulled up the files they'd need on her laptop.

"You can grab Willow's chair until she comes back," Kennedy offered. "It should only take me a minute."

"Isn't this yours?" Kennedy heard the smile in Reuben's expression before she glanced over at him. "I thought you said you lost it."

She reached out for the phone he dangled between his fingers. "Hey, where was that?"

"Right here on your roommate's desk. I knew it couldn't be hers. She isn't the type to have John 3:16 on her phone case."

"No, I wouldn't," Willow remarked from the doorway.

Kennedy put the cell in her bag. "Reuben just found my phone on your desk."

"Huh." Willow shrugged. "All kinds of mysteries today."

"What other mysteries?" Kennedy asked automatically even though she was focused more on getting her file downloaded.

In her periphery, she saw Willow fling her hair over her shoulder. "I left around noon to find some breakfast. I know

I locked up."

Kennedy pressed print and wondered if Willow's story had a point or if maybe she simply appreciated having a male audience member paying attention to her.

"Well, when I came back ..."

"Let me guess," Reuben interrupted. "Your door was wide open."

Willow pouted. "No. But it was unlocked. And I know for sure I locked it up."

Kennedy shrugged. "I've done that before. Maybe we should mention it to the RA. Might be the lock itself."

"Oooh," Willow exclaimed, "let me be the one to tell him. I've been dying for an excuse to stop by his room."

"You'd be better off going to Fatima. You know, the RA for the girls' hall?"

Willow shrugged. "The other one's cuter."

Kennedy rolled her eyes, and Reuben stifled a chuckle. "What?" Willow asked. "Just because he's a junior you think I can't get his attention?"

Kennedy snatched the pages from her printer. "Come on," she told Reuben. "Let's get this lab finished up, now that we've wasted half the afternoon."

"What?" Willow demanded. "You still don't think ..."

Kennedy's ringtone interrupted Willow's tirade. "Is that

mine?" she asked, digging it out of her backpack. "I thought the batteries were dead."

"Guess it's your lucky day." Reuben headed for the stairs and Kennedy followed him out.

She didn't recognize the caller ID. "Hello?"

"Kennedy, honey, it's me, Sandy. I forgot to give you the cookies I made for you earlier. We were going to stop by and surprise you, but Carl lost the address you wrote for him."

"I didn't lose it," Kennedy could hear Carl object in the background. "I had it right here on the desk. On a purple Post-it."

"Well, anyway," Sandy breezed over him, "are you at your dorm now? Because I want you to have them while they're fresh. If I had been in my right mind, I would have sent them back with you this afternoon, but, you know …"

Sandy's voice trailed off. As Kennedy walked toward the library with Reuben, she searched for something to say to keep Sandy from feeling guilty over homemade goodies. "That's really sweet of you. I'm actually getting ready to work on a lab report, but if you give me a call when you're pulling up to campus I can come out to the parking lot and meet you."

"I'm sorry we couldn't surprise you, sweetie. But you know Carl, always misplacing everything …"

Carl's flustered reply was barely audible.

"Well, I'll see you pretty soon." Sandy's voice rang out strong and melodic. "We just have to finish up these postcards."

Kennedy was glad to note how much more chipper Sandy sounded compared to earlier.

"You know," Sandy continued, "I feel awful about this afternoon. Here you are, I haven't seen you since you were in my Sunday school class way back when, and we didn't even get to have a proper how-you-doing chat."

"Well, I know today's been a crazy day," Kennedy began and then stopped, reluctant to bring up the incident at the center.

"Don't you worry about us," Sandy prattled. "You know, Carl and I, we've been through hell and back more times than you've been around the sun. We're just thankful you weren't hurt, honey. And you weren't too shook up, were you?"

"I'm all right," Kennedy assured her, although thinking about that afternoon made her shiver in the autumn breeze. By the time Sandy was done talking, Kennedy and Reuben were already stepping up to the library.

Reuben held the door open. "That woman has a loud voice."

"That's the pastor's wife at the church I checked out this morning. I knew her a long time ago, before we moved."

Reuben didn't say anything else as they made their way to their regular study spot near the art history books.

"So, you want to talk?" Reuben asked when they both sat down.

"Talk about what?"

"Whatever happened today. Why you were so late. Why you started shaking on the phone just now."

"I wasn't shaking." Kennedy laughed nervously.

"Yes, you were. You want to talk?" he asked again.

She glanced at their books on the table. "Not really."

Reuben leaned back in his chair, crossed his arms, and studied her. "All right. Then let's take a look at that lab."

They finished up their report a few hours later over dinner. Reuben even managed to keep from spilling anything on their paper or getting dirty finger smears on any of the pages.

"You doing anything else tonight?" he asked as they walked together back toward Kennedy's dorm.

"I have to read a little more Dostoevsky. But that's pretty relaxing."

Reuben chuckled.

"What's so funny?"

"Not many people use *Dostoevsky* and *relaxing* in the same sentence, I imagine."

They said good-night, and Kennedy's legs felt as heavy as titanium as she trudged up the stairs. She was glad Willow was out. She could use some quiet time to herself. She gathered up her robe and shower supplies when her phone rang. *Not again.* She glanced at the time. It could be her mother. She groaned and put down her towel when she saw the number. She had been so busy with Reuben she'd completely forgotten about those silly cookies.

"Hi, Sandy," she sighed, trying to muster up some convincing resemblance to enthusiasm.

"Kennedy, it's me." When she heard the tension in Carl's voice, Kennedy overlooked her own exhaustion.

"Did you find out who the girl is?" She clutched the phone to her ear.

"No," Carl answered. "No, Sandy wanted me to tell you she's terribly sorry about the cookies."

Disappointment sank to the floor of Kennedy's gut like a concrete ball.

On the other line, she could hear Carl sigh, too. "We're just now leaving the center, believe it or not. We had the police to talk to, they went over the whole joint, then the reporters …"

"It's all right. Tell Sandy I just had dinner, and I'm stuffed now, anyway."

"Well, she's still planning to get these cookies to you."

Kennedy wondered if maybe she should feign a diet or something so the Lindgrens would stop worrying. The gesture was nice, but Kennedy couldn't imagine how fretting over a plate of sweets could be beneficial to their health.

"Anyway…" Carl let out a nervous-sounding chuckle. "The reporters are wondering who's really behind the vandalism. One suggested Wayne may have planned it to garnish extra publicity."

Kennedy's whole face scrunched up at the thought of the politician. "Do they have any proof?"

"You know how reporters are," Carl answered. "Act like they're holding all the cards and you never know if they're bluffing until you see it all in print."

Kennedy didn't know much of anything about reporters, but she was sorry the Lindgrens had gone through so much today.

"Well, I don't want to bother you," Carl said. "I should let you go. Sandy just wants me to say she'll call you tomorrow about the cookies. We can't have her baking go to waste, you know."

Kennedy told Carl good-night and ended the call as her low battery light came on. That was weird. It was over halfway charged when Reuben found it that afternoon. She plugged it in and reminded herself to talk to her dad. Maybe it was time for a new battery or something.

She picked up her towel and stared around the room. What was it about being alone that made the back of her neck prickle? Had she gotten so used to having others around that solitude freaked her out and left her skin all covered in goose bumps? She glanced at the window to make sure the blinds were down, half expecting to see someone staring right at her.

What a crazy day. As she headed to the showers, she hoped tomorrow would be a little calmer.

CHAPTER 9

Exhaustion clung to Kennedy's limbs when her alarm rang Monday morning. She wasn't much of a coffee drinker but decided she might stop for something on the way to lab. Her roommate didn't have any classes before noon, at least none she regularly attended, so Kennedy got dressed as quietly as she could with the light from her desk lamp. Her phone beeped, and she hoped it wasn't a text from Reuben saying there was a mistake in their lab. They had to submit it in fifteen minutes. She looked at the message.

This is Nick from church. I have a question about that call you got.

How in the world was she supposed to concentrate on science after getting a text like that? Well, he'd have to save it for later. She started typing to tell him she was off to class but stopped. Lab wasn't over until noon. Could she really wait that long? Would she be able to focus on anything besides Rose? She was halfway down the stairs before she decided to call him back.

"Hey, Kennedy," he answered. "I got your number from Carl. Hope I didn't wake you up or anything."

"No, I'm on my way to class, though, so I only have a minute."

He made a sound like smacking his lips together. "Well, I started browsing through our youth group roster when I came in this morning. We don't have anyone named Rose, but if we assume she used a fake name, it looks like there are two girls who may or may not be our mystery caller."

Hope swelled in Kennedy's chest like an over-inflated balloon.

"Unfortunately, neither one is a perfect match."

Pop.

"One is a homeschool girl who's actually fourteen now. And the other is thirteen and *was* homeschooled until this fall when her parents enrolled her in private school."

Kennedy slowed down her pace as the science complex loomed into view.

"Like I said," Nick went on, "neither one is a perfect fit."

Kennedy sighed. Out of all the girls at St. Margaret's …

"Well, thanks for looking." She tried not to let the disappointment creep into her voice.

"Wait a minute," Nick went on. "See, both the girls were in a drama last spring. We've got the whole thing on video. I was thinking, if you wanted to meet me here at the church I could show you the recording. Do you think if you heard her voice, you'd be able to tell if it was the girl you talked to?"

Kennedy knew for a fact she could replicate Rose's voice even in her sleep, since that's all she had done last night in her dreams. "Yeah, I could probably do that."

"I'm here until three and then I'm off to one of the elementary schools for Good News Club," Nick said. "Do you have time to come on by?"

"I can take the T and be there by about one." Kennedy's backpack hung heavy on her shoulders when she thought about the full schedule ahead. "Would that give us enough time?"

"Sounds perfect." She could hear Nick's smile from the other end of the line.

"Ok, talk to you then." She went to push the end button and saw her phone was already back down to half a battery after charging all night. Yeah, she definitely had to talk to her dad about a replacement. If she could find the time to get hold of him, that is. Kennedy wondered if her classmates from the East Coast realized how fortunate they were that they didn't have to worry about time-zone issues.

Kennedy saw Reuben waiting for her at the door to the science building and sped up. She probably wasn't any closer to figuring out who Rose was, but at least others were asking questions, trying to help.

The three hours of lab passed faster than they might have thanks to Reuben's good nature and humor. For bits at a time, Kennedy forgot about the pregnancy center and her upcoming meeting with Nick. She found herself laughing with Reuben on her way out of class, and part of her wished Carl had never asked her to get involved at the center in the first place. She was here at Harvard for her education, and if it hadn't been for some fortunate miracle and her lab partner's charming personality, she couldn't have made it through the past few hours without completely losing her focus. She was beginning to think that even if she had time for pregnancy center ministry, she didn't have the emotional capacity to juggle it along with her schoolwork.

"Want to grab some lunch?" Reuben asked. "I need to study more for calculus."

"I can't, I'm off to St. Margaret's, that church I visited. I have a meeting there."

"You're not in trouble, are you?" Reuben asked, his tone almost defensive.

Kennedy laughed. "No, nothing like that. We're still

trying to see if there's any way we can figure out who called us the other night."

"That's still got you worried, doesn't it?"

She nodded. "Last night I kept jerking myself awake. I kept thinking I heard the hotline phone ringing again," she admitted with a chuckle.

"It's because you've got a big heart, my friend."

Kennedy glanced at Reuben, expecting to see his familiar sarcastic grin, but his expression was warm, considerate.

He stuck his hands in his pockets. "You know you can always come knock on my door if you need anything."

"Thanks." She forced a smile so he wouldn't think she was depressed on top of crazy. "I really appreciate that."

"What are friends for?" He elbowed her playfully on the side of her arm, and that old crooked grin spread across his face once more.

"I better go," she told him.

The underground T station was nearly as dark as a solar eclipse compared to the bright midday sun. Kennedy paid for her token and stood on the platform to wait. She hadn't expected to get so nervous. What if she heard one of the girls on the video and recognized Rose's voice? They could go to the police. They'd have enough evidence to warrant an investigation, right? Especially if Carl got behind them. Maybe he could talk Wayne Abernathy into using his political sway to get the case open. But what if the girl's uncle had already taken her to an abortion clinic? What if they were too late? Kennedy's stomach tried flipping itself inside out every time she thought about it. Who would be sick and depraved enough to violate ...

"Excuse me. Did you drop your book?" Someone tapped her back, and a man in sunglasses held out a paperback novel. There was a small scar running from his thumb joint to his wrist. She scanned the cover. Historical, by the looks of it, with a pretty long-haired brunette wearing a velvet gown on the cover, something Kennedy's mom might like. "No, that's not mine. Thank you, though."

He shrugged and went on. Kennedy wondered when she'd have time to start the next mystery her mom ordered her from Amazon. She glanced at the clock in the subway station. If she had planned ahead, she would have brought *Crime and Punishment* to read while she waited.

The redline train finally arrived, and after the short ride, Kennedy walked the last few blocks to the church. Her insides trembled a little when she stepped into St. Margaret's again. Some kind of psychosomatic response, she told herself and ignored the uncomfortable quivering. She was wearing a long-sleeved blouse covered by a loose sweater. At least Nick wouldn't see how much she was shaking.

She sped up as she neared his office. Now she was there, she wanted to look at the videos and leave. Nick's door was slightly ajar, but she knocked anyway and waited for him to call her in. He was wearing a T-shirt with a picture of Jesus smiling and drinking a Coke. "Boy, you look tired," he exclaimed.

She gave him a surprised look, and they both laughed.

"I'm sorry. Let me try that again." Nick cleared his throat. "Kennedy, hi. How are you? Do you want some coffee?"

Kennedy accepted his offer. She knew she must look as awful as she felt. To complete the picture, she had accidentally fallen asleep last night with her contacts in, and her eyes were now bright red as well as itchy. She couldn't remember the brand of eye-drops her dad got her the last time that happened, and she added it to her list of questions to ask him.

"So, I got the video up." Nick fidgeted with his pen. "Unfortunately, I watched it again, and Harmony has a few lines, but Alicia doesn't actually talk." He slid the cursor until somewhere about halfway through the video. "All right, here's where we hear Harmony."

He pointed his pen to a confident-looking teenager on the side of the screen who exclaimed in a melodramatic voice, *"I don't see why we have to do anything for her at all."* The audio was pretty poor quality, but Kennedy shook her head right away.

"That's not her." The girl in the recording was bold. Outspoken. She could handle the spotlight in a way Rose almost certainly couldn't.

"All right. That was easy." Nick scrolled to another part of the video and leaned forward. "Well, here's what Alicia looks like. You can see her there behind that boy with the mike."

Kennedy squinted at the screen.

"If I remember right," Nick continued, "she'll come up front a little bit later in the show so you can get a better look."

He skipped ahead. "There. This gives a pretty good picture. I just wish we could hear her voice."

Kennedy frowned at the image. "Is this the highest resolution you've got?"

"Yeah, sorry about that."

She leaned forward. The girl wasn't as petite as Kennedy pictured Rose, but there was a shy look in her eyes. "Would you say she's pretty quiet?" Kennedy asked.

Nick nodded. "Yeah. Unless she's with her brothers or sisters. Those kids are like little Shriners when they get together, just without the hats."

"Shriners?"

"You know, those funny guys in parades ..."

The last parade Kennedy had seen was when she was about six, but she didn't say anything. It was just another one of those cultural references any other American her age would catch onto right away. Just another reminder she wasn't quite at home at Harvard as she hoped.

"Anyway," Nick went on, "Alicia's pretty quiet when she's by herself, but she can get rowdy when she's with her brothers and sisters. Her mom just had a new baby if I remember right. Makes nine or ten altogether now."

Kennedy had grown up as an only child and couldn't imagine that many kids running around one house. "And she's the one who's fourteen?"

"Yeah."

Kennedy peered at the photo one last time. Could you tell if a person was abused or not just by looking at a picture?

"Good family, you'd say?" she prodded.

"Yeah, I think so. Carl knows them pretty well."

"She said she was thirteen on the phone."

Nick shrugged. "I just thought it was worth mentioning, since their whole family is homeschooled."

Kennedy didn't say anything but sat staring at the monitor. There were at least a dozen girls on stage. Why couldn't one of them be Rose?

"That's not her, is it?" Nick finally asked.

She let out her breath. "I don't know. Part of me wants it to be, but ..."

He clicked off the monitor. "Yeah, I didn't think so, either."

They looked at each other for a moment. Kennedy knew she should go, but she was so tired.

"I know you're busy with school," Nick added tentatively, "but we have youth group on Tuesday nights. If you wanted to come by tomorrow, I could introduce you as a new helper for the junior high girls ..."

"What? Go in undercover?" Kennedy chuckled even though she didn't find the situation at all humorous. She wondered what her parents would say about the whole situation. Would they be proud of her trying to protect someone so helpless and vulnerable as Rose? Or would they tell her to mind her own business and focus on her studies? She had the feeling they would approve of her volunteer work until her grades started to suffer for it. She had already spent Friday afternoon at the center and Sunday at St. Margaret's. Now she was here again, and Nick was talking about her coming back tomorrow for youth group.

"I'm not sure," she confessed. "I really wasn't planning to get this involved in the first place."

"Yeah." Nick drummed the pen against his desk. "I know. Carl's really stressed out about it all, too, what with the election and everything coming up."

"What's the election have to do with it?" Kennedy asked. Two months in the States and she was already sick of American politics.

"Well, Abernathy is a high-profile candidate. Lots of people love him. And just as many hate him. We've had journalists poking around, attending services, asking Carl questions."

"I didn't even realize he attended here. I thought he just showed up yesterday to pray."

"No." Nick stretched his arms behind his head and leaned back in his chair. "His family's been coming here for years. He and Carl knew each other back in college, or something like that."

"Where is Carl?" Kennedy asked, looking around as if talking about him should make him materialize in the doorway.

"It's his day off. Well, technically, at least," Nick answered. "I think he and Sandy are cleaning up the center. I guess there was a lot of graffiti ..."

"I was there." Kennedy didn't want to remember those slogans on the wall. If she didn't have her Russian literature class later in the afternoon, she could stop by Elm Street and offer to help. Why couldn't there be an extra five or ten hours packed into every day? She stood with a sigh. "Well, thanks for showing me the video."

"Yeah, no problem." Nick stood up awkwardly, as if his body didn't know if he wanted to take the extra steps to walk around the desk or if he would see her out from where he was. He held up his hand. "Thanks for coming in. Sorry we didn't ..." He frowned. "Sorry it didn't work out. But God knows where she is, right?"

Kennedy forced a smile even though his words were a little too optimistic for her current mood.

God, if you know where she is, how hard would it be for you to give us a little clue?

She hugged her sweater tighter across her chest as she headed back out into the brisk autumn afternoon.

CHAPTER 10

Once Kennedy got back to her dorm, she spent half an hour before class studying for the next day's calculus test. She munched on dry Cheerios and thought about her meeting with Nick while she worked on her practice problems.

St. Margaret's was a big church. Why should it be so hard to find one girl? There should be at least a few dozen families who homeschooled, right? And none of them had a thirteen-year-old daughter? It didn't make sense.

When it was time for her to close her books and head to her Russian lit class, she still wasn't any closer to an answer. Maybe she should call Carl, see what he said. She had gone over her phone conversations with Rose hundreds of times already. Had she forgotten something — one little detail that could solve the whole mystery? During class, she listed each particular she could remember about the phone call and only heard half of what the professor said.

Reuben texted her that evening to see if she wanted to

study math over dinner, but she feigned a headache and went back to her room. She really would have a migraine by the end of the night if she kept this up. She plopped down in her desk chair and heaved open her huge calculus book.

She gaped at the first problem for over ten minutes before she finally gave up. Maybe she should email her mom. Kennedy opened up her inbox. After gazing at the screen for another few minutes without typing anything, she finally shook her head and went to the St. Margaret's website. There had to be some kind of clue.

There was a little search box on top of the home page. Kennedy knew she wouldn't get any hits, but she typed in *Rose* anyway and waited for the computer to tell her the search term hadn't been found. She was wasting time. She still had to spend another hour or so on her practice problems if she wanted to be ready for her calculus test tomorrow, and she was now officially behind in *Crime and Punishment*, which she needed to finish in a week along with a ten-page research paper.

She followed the links to the photos page. There were plenty of pictures from the youth group, even though none of students' names was listed. What was she doing? Did she really expect staring at photos of strangers would help?

Besides, if Rose was part of Nick's youth group, wouldn't he have been able to identify her?

But what if Rose only came to St. Margaret's with her family on Sundays? It would be impossible for anybody at a church that size to know everyone else. So how in the world could they find her? She thought for a moment about calling Carl, but he had been through so much the past two days. Now he and Sandy were probably going crazy trying to get everything ready for Thursday's dinner to celebrate the center's opening. It was going to be fancy, and having Senator Abernathy speak would draw a lot of people in as well, she suspected.

Some music. That's what she needed to focus. She typed in the address for her favorite online radio station. She still had to get those calculus problems finished.

The website loaded slowly, so she went back to the St. Margaret's page while she waited. She had taken almost all Advanced Placement classes during her senior year in Yanji and still graduated with a 4.0. So far at Harvard, she hadn't gotten lower than a 92 on any test or assignment. She could handle culture shock, weekly lab write-ups, and still find time to read a mystery or two a month. Why couldn't she track down a single girl? It wasn't like the city was overrun with homeschooled thirteen-year-olds named Rose. Maybe she would take Nick's suggestion and visit the youth group tomorrow night. Her study group was meeting until about 5:30. What time did Nick say she should come?

She clicked on the St. Margaret's calendar of events. *Youth group. Tuesday night, seven to nine.* Well, she might make it. If she wasn't already behind in every single class by then.

Something on the bottom of the calendar caught her eye. *Homeschool group field trip. Tour of the State House.* Straightening up in her chair, Kennedy searched to see if there was more information about the homeschool group. She finally found a quick blurb under the women's ministry tab:

Our mission is to provide support to the homeschooling families in our congregation. We offer fellowship through field trips, cooperative learning experiences, and a quarterly homeschool moms' support group. Contact Vivian Abernathy for details.

Abernathy? What if ...? No, it couldn't be ... She did a quick google search for Wayne Abernathy. Her computer was running slower than normal, but by the time the image of his family finished loading, she had already read the caption.

Wayne and Vivian Abernathy with their two children, Noah (age 16) and Jodie (age 12).

Kennedy's pulse was the only thing in the room racing faster than her mind. The picture was dated. She quickly counted back. Nine months ago. She stared at the family. Vivian was tall, a woman who was obviously aging but still trying to cling to the last remnants of her youth. She had her arm around her son, who stood with a half-smile that made Kennedy guess he would rather be anywhere than posing for one of his father's campaign photos. The fingers on Vivian Abernathy's other hand intertwined tenderly with her daughter's wind-blown bits of hair. Kennedy looked at the name again. *Jodie.* She was quite a bit shorter and even more petite than her mom, as if a strong wind might erase her from memory. Her clothes were pressed and elegant, and her pearl earrings looked out of place on someone so young. Kennedy studied the smile and tried to guess if she was a happy child or not.

Jodie. Was it possible …?

There were footsteps outside her door. Voices. The sun was almost down, and Kennedy hadn't turned on the lights. Her eyeballs were jabbing pain to the back of her brain after staring so much. How long had she been sleuthing behind her computer screen?

The door burst open, and Kennedy gave a little start. "Oh, it's you." She let out her breath when Willow came in.

"I thought you were at rehearsal."

"I will be." Willow's voice was always dramatic but now had a strange sort of drawl to it. She walked lazily to her dresser and pulled out some nightclothes. "Don't wait up for me tonight, ok? I'll just take what I need and see you tomorrow."

Kennedy rolled her eyes when Willow burped.

"Don't you want to know who it is?" Willow hunched over and slumped an arm on the back of Kennedy's chair. "The RA from the other hall. I told you I was going to talk to him about that lock, right?"

Her roommate's breath reeked, but Kennedy didn't make any comments. It wouldn't be the first time Willow spent the night away.

"Good-night," she muttered as Willow hummed her way out of the room, leaving the door a crack open.

As soon Willow was gone, Kennedy started browsing Wayne Abernathy's personal webpage. A lot of the information had to do with the upcoming election, but it did include a brief bio. Married to Vivian, a lawyer before she left the workplace to raise their children. The page didn't say much about the kids but did give updated ages. *Jodie R. Abernathy, 13 years old.*

Something told Kennedy to exit out of her browser. This

wasn't going to lead her anywhere, all this speculation. What good would it do? She needed to get to work on her calculus. She tried to guess what Carl would say if he knew what she was doing, knew what she was thinking. She should stick to reading Russian crime novels, not inventing her own conspiracies. Was she really that desperate to find Rose?

Her fingers were as stubborn as her mind, however, and they refused to slow down. *Jodie Abernathy,* she typed into the search bar, leaning forward in her seat as she scrolled through the results. Halfway down the second page, she froze.

Jodie Rose Abernathy, daughter of State House ...

Rose.

She didn't click the link. She didn't touch the mouse. She held her breath and felt like she might swallow her own heart. Suddenly, she wished Willow hadn't left for the night. She wished her parents didn't live on the other side of the world. She wished she wasn't alone in her room. She reached down for her backpack.

She had to call Carl.

But she never got the chance.

CHAPTER 11

"Is this Willow's room?"

Kennedy managed to swallow down a full-fledged scream and only made a little yelp when her door banged open. She had never seen the student before. He wore a long-sleeved flannel shirt and stared around the room wildly.

"Who are you?"

"Dustin. Are you Willow's roommate?"

Why didn't Willow ever pull the door completely shut? Kennedy sighed. "Yeah." She exited out of the webpages, and when a flush warmed up her face, she reminded herself she hadn't done anything illegal or shameful.

The stranger's eyes were everywhere at once and he scanned one side of the room to another. "There's been an accident. Do you know where her wallet is?"

Kennedy stood up only to remember she hadn't eaten anything since lunch except for some dry Cheerios. She put her hand on the back of her chair to steady herself. "What kind of accident?"

"She was hit by a car just a few minutes ago. The ambulance is on its way. They need her ID."

"I'll look." Kennedy had no idea where it was, but she felt better about going through her roommate's personal effects than letting someone else do it. Willow's top drawer had a journal Kennedy had never seen her write in, some homeopathic cough drops, a few sticks of unburned incense, and a picture of her hiking with some friends up a snow-capped mountain back home in Alaska. No ID anywhere.

Dustin rummaged through the things on top of Willow's desk. "Here. This must be her wallet." He slipped it in his pocket. "Do you ... I mean, she's your roommate. Do you want me to show you ...?"

Kennedy was already slipping on her shoes.

"She was at the crosswalk. The car came out of nowhere." He bounded down the stairs two at a time.

"You saw it?" Kennedy had to run to keep up.

"Yeah. Wicked crazy." Dustin looked back at Kennedy over his shoulder as they hurried past the dorms. "I hope she's ok. Are you guys close?"

Kennedy wondered how to answer that question. Willow and she didn't share any of the same moral values, but they respected each other's space and so far had co-existed just fine. A few times they even streamed an action movie on Willow's desktop to watch together. "Yeah, I guess so."

"Well, I'm really sorry." He froze. "I don't see the ambulance. Maybe they already got her to the hospital."

"What was wrong with her?" Kennedy wasn't sure she really wanted to know.

"I didn't see everything, but it looked pretty bad." Dustin pointed ahead. "I think I see one of the cars that stopped to help her. Let me go ask him what the paramedics said."

Kennedy jogged after him. When she caught up, he was bending over, talking to the driver through the open window. "This is her roommate." He turned to Kennedy. "There's a guy in the backseat who wants to ask you something." He opened the door, and Kennedy peered in.

"There's no one back there."

Before she could react, Dustin elbowed her in the ribs. She doubled over. He grabbed her shoulder. Air. She needed a little air. Then she would yell for help. She tried to gasp.

Strong, sharp fingers pressed into the back of her neck. She flailed out her arms, trying to remember those dumb self-defense videos her dad made her watch. How could she go for the eyes if she couldn't even keep her balance?

Her lungs filled noisily with air. "Help!"

Dustin kicked her hard in the belly. She fell into the

backseat and immediately stopped struggling when he brought a small knife just centimeters from her chest.

"Shut up."

She took shallow breaths. Dustin put one leg into the car, and she scrambled backward away from him.

"Hold still," he ordered.

She bit her lips together to keep from squealing. *Breathe evenly.* She could almost hear her dad's voice. Back when she lived in Yanji, she thought his emphasis on crisis preparation was one of his strange, morbid quirks. How many other girls at her high school actually had to role-play kidnapping scenarios? At the time, Kennedy thought it had something to do with her dad's paranoia about being an American overseas. He seized the stories of one or two US businessmen getting captured for ransom and created a whole atmosphere of fear. Now, she was grateful for his words in her head.

Create as much noise as you can during the abduction itself. Well, that had failed. All she got out was one pitiful yelp. If making a scene didn't help, the best thing to do was stay calm. *They're going to be tense. You don't want to make them even more nervous.*

And so she sat as the car sped onto the road. When Dustin covered her eyes with a blindfold, she didn't resist. She tried not to wince when he raised her hands over her head and cuffed her wrists to the neck-rest behind her. When the car made its first turn, she counted her breaths. Over and over and over. Someone would come. Someone would free her. This wasn't China, with its corrupt police force and neo-communist justice system. This was America. God wouldn't allow them to actually hurt her. He couldn't. Her parents were missionaries. She had grown up singing praises in Sunday school. People prayed for her. People admired her. She wasn't the kind of person who could just disappear.

She shut her eyes, which made her feel a little less powerless in the blindfold. If it was going to be dark, it was going to be dark because she wanted it to be. She clung to her dad's words as if they were a personal guarantee of her own safety. *If they want a ransom, they have no reason to harm you.*

The car sped ahead as if nothing had happened. The man in the front said something to Dustin. Kennedy strained her ears. She had to pay attention. She could tell the police what their voices sounded like ...

But what would that do? She remembered her 911 conversation last weekend. The people there couldn't even trace a simple phone call. Besides, how did she expect them to rescue her when nobody knew she was gone?

The realization hit her in the gut like a cannonball, sending splinters of fear and dread and disbelief coursing through her being. *Nobody knew she was gone.* She took a deep breath.

This was going to be the longest night of her life.

Assuming she survived until morning.

CHAPTER 12

"My parents live in China. My dad has a printing business there."

Kennedy knew she was rambling but couldn't stop the torrent of words from flowing out her mouth. She wanted them to know she was a real person, not a nameless victim. And if they were after money, she wanted them to accurately estimate what her family might or might not be able to afford. She tried to keep from thinking about her mom and how freaked out she would be to get a ransom call from overseas.

"I have a roommate." Kennedy was still blindfolded, but she turned to Dustin next to her. "She'll wonder where I am if I'm not back tonight." Did her voice sound convincing enough, or could he tell she was lying? Willow was out with her newest interest and wouldn't be back until sometime tomorrow. Kennedy could be gone for twenty-four hours or more before Willow started to get suspicious.

"I have a boyfriend." That was a lie too, but it sounded better than calling Reuben her lab partner. "We're supposed to meet in half an hour to study for a test." It didn't matter if that wasn't true, either. These men had to understand their plans would backfire. They had to understand she wasn't the kind of person someone could pluck off the streets and get away with it.

"You're going to text your roommate *and* your boyfriend." The driver in front had one of those heavy Boston accents Kennedy had previously thought were only from movies. "You're going to tell them your aunt in Maryland broke her hip and your parents begged you to go check on her."

Kennedy's blood froze and her hands chilled at the mention of her aunt Lilian. How could they know? She thought about when Dustin came bursting into her room and called Willow by name. They had obviously planned ahead. But why?

"I don't have my phone with me." Remembering all her dad's advice, she tried to keep her expression neutral. She didn't want to make them angry.

"We do." Dustin's voice was younger, not as gruff as the driver's. He poked her in the side with something small.

"You have my phone?" How had they managed that?

Dustin had stayed on Willow's side of the room the entire time. Were these magicians and illusionists she was dealing with?

"It's a copy, stupid."

Flashes of the previous day flickered in her memory. Her lost phone. The fire drill.

"How can I text when I'm cuffed to the seat?" Kennedy tried to guess how fast the car was moving. If they freed her hands to write a message, could she dive out? And if she did, would she roll right into oncoming traffic?

"Don't give her the phone, idiot," the driver spat. "Do it for her."

She listened while Dustin typed on her phone, or the copy of it — another curiosity she had previously thought only came from movies.

A minute later, the phone beeped. "Reuben wants to know if you uploaded your titration results to the class database yet. Whatever that means."

"Yeah, I did it this afternoon." Kennedy tried to picture her dad's comforting face. Maybe if she pretended this was some role-playing test he had designed for her …

From the front seat, the driver grumbled something or other about traffic. It was rush hour. Were they going out of the city, then, stuck in a sea of commuters?

The phone beeped again a few minutes later. "Willow says do you mind if someone sleeps in your bed while you're gone."

Her bed. The one she wasn't in right now. Would she ever see it again?

"Forget about that," the driver called back. "Who else do you need to contact?" he asked Kennedy. She felt the car turn. Was this the second or third right so far?

"I have a calculus test tomorrow. Then I have general chemistry."

"I don't need your whole stinking schedule," he interrupted. "Just tell me who's gonna miss you if you don't check in."

The more Kennedy thought about it, the more she realized Reuben and Willow were the only people who would care if she vanished. Had she really spent two whole months at Harvard and not made any other friends?

"My parents." Would her kidnappers let her call her parents? She tried to think of some sort of code, some way she could tell them she was in trouble. Her dad had come up with contingency plans in case the Chinese police raided their home in the middle of the night. Couldn't he have dreamed up a secret phrase to signal distress? If these men let her phone Yanji …

"We already sent your mom an email," Dustin said. "You're incredibly busy studying, plus you have laryngitis so you can't call. Easy."

So they had access to her email, too. "Who are you?"

"Just shut up," the driver mumbled.

She had lost track of the turns by now and wondered if they were driving around in circles. She strained her ears to try to detect any background noise that might clue her in to her surroundings, but all she could hear were the generic sounds of traffic. That, plus the roar of her own pulse in her ears. At one point, she was certain she heard the faintest hint of a police siren, but it disappeared faster than a lightning flash.

And so she was left alone with her thoughts. Her thoughts, her fears, her racing heart. Were they going to hurt her? Were they going to kill her? They knew her roommate. They had access to her phone and emails. Why? If her parents were billionaires or something, it would make sense for someone to go to such lengths to track her. Hunt her down. But all this for the daughter of an overseas printer? Could it have something to do with her parents' secret missionary work in China, then? If it were a movie, she'd joke with her dad about how far-fetched and contrived it all was.

Her eyes were still shut, and she figured her dad would try to tell her to let her body rest. What was that about sexual predators and their first goal was to tire you out? But would these men really go through so much trouble just for …

"My pastor will miss me," she blurted out. "We've been working on a …" She didn't want to mention anything about the hotline phone. "We've been working on a big fundraising dinner for Thursday. He'll be expecting to hear from me."

"Not no more. You've already sent Carl a text telling him you have laryngitis and a research paper to work on all week."

So they knew about her pastor, too? Who were they? Kennedy's one ray of hope was that Sandy would see the text about the laryngitis and bring over some chicken soup or those ridiculous cookies she kept talking about. Otherwise it could be days, maybe a week or more, before someone reported her disappearance. What horrors would she endure in the meantime?

Would they even keep her alive that long?

She guessed about an hour passed before they parked, but she didn't know if the terror or the blindfold were playing tricks with her mind. It was breezy when they forced her out of the car. She strained her ears for clues about where she was. Why couldn't there be a train? Something to tell her where she was? Were they still in Massachusetts? The ground was hard. Pavement. That was a good sign, right? At least they weren't out in the middle of the woods where search parties could hunt for weeks and still find nothing. But if she got a chance to run, would there be any place to hide?

There were no sounds, no cars, no traffic. She imagined that some people in her position might call for help in case anyone was nearby, but she could hardly muster the strength to support her own weight. "Where are we?" Her voice was quiet, squeaky. She wondered if this was how Rose felt when she made that call on the hotline phone.

Rose. Was all that a dream? Had she made it all up? Could Rose really be Jodie Abernathy? Sitting behind her computer desk, Kennedy had been so certain. The age, the middle name, the homeschool connection. But now it all seemed so distant, so jumbled. Even if Rose was Wayne Abernathy's daughter, that still didn't explain why Kennedy was abducted, miles from her dorm, uncertain if she'd survive the night.

Unless ...

They started to walk, and Kennedy shoved thoughts of Rose aside. She had one goal — to stay alive. Once she returned safe and sound to her Harvard dorm, she would talk to Carl about her suspicions.

If she returned.

She heard the sound of something lifting, a garage door or something as heavy. "Go on." When it closed behind them again, the ground reverberated, and its thud echoed around the room. No, she couldn't escape out that way.

Her hands were still cuffed, and she raised them in front of her to keep from bumping into anything. She tried counting how many steps they were taking her, but her pulse was roaring far too loudly in her ears and she lost track. A trained detective might be able to listen to her accosters' footsteps and discern the exact size and style of shoe they wore, but Kennedy was clueless. Besides, how in the world would it help her escape to know if her abductor wore a size ten or size thirteen?

They descended a staircase, and the air grew even chillier. She guessed if they let her look she would see her own breath, choppy as it was. She tried to rub her hands together, but her wrists chafed on the cuffs. She couldn't feel any railings to either side of her and was afraid of tripping.

"Watch your step." She recognized Dustin's voice and actually welcomed his hand on her bicep. His grip was forceful, but it almost felt as if he were holding her, supporting her quivering legs, preparing to catch her if she lost her balance.

When they reached the bottom of the stairs, the gnawing feeling in her stomach had grown until her entire abdominal cavity was a vacuum, void of life, void of emotion, void of matter. They slowed to a stop.

"Sit here."

Kennedy's shin bumped a couch. She felt the scratchy fabric with her hands and turned her face away from the musty smell. How long had it been rotting down here? How many other victims had used it before? Was she alone? She pictured herself in a room as cold and bleak and empty as the holodecks in those sci-fi shows she sometimes watched with her dad. Blackness. On and on forever even though your body was in a room, enclosed by four walls. She lowered herself carefully onto the couch, half expecting a rodent to come scampering out from underneath, ready to complain at whoever disturbed his rest.

Someone grabbed her wrists. His hands were warm. Didn't he know it was below freezing down here? She might die of exposure if nothing else.

She let out her breath when he unlocked the left side of the cuff. She forced herself to thank him, but her voice was still so small, so scared. Had her dad known? When he dragged her through all those seemingly pointless training scenarios, when he grilled her about how she'd respond if she was ever abducted, did he know how small she would sound?

Unfortunately, the man with the warm hands didn't take off her other cuff but attached it to something metallic sticking out of the wall behind. She wanted to argue. They could trust her. She would cooperate. She wouldn't run. But they'd know she was lying. She reached up to finger her blindfold.

"Don't." It was Dustin's voice.

She let her free hand drop to her lap.

"That's better."

Should she bother to scream? Other than the knife he pulled to get her in the car, she hadn't noticed any other weapons. No guns to her temple like in a thriller novel. No long blades pressed up against her jugular. The men hadn't talked to anyone else since they came in. Were they the only two guarding her?

She licked her dry lips. What did it matter? Two men or fifty, she wasn't getting out of here. Not yet. But still, if they weren't armed, wouldn't that make a rescue attempt a whole lot more likely to succeed?

She heard the men shuffle away, listened to the rumble of

their voices as they conversed in a low murmur somewhere far off. Were they deciding what to do with her?

She wished her father hadn't told her so many statistics about abducted women and what might happen to them. Which horrible fate would she face? A lifetime of slavery in an underground sex ring? Or would she end up in a freezer, cut into pieces and stuffed into bloody Ziploc bags? Would they find her next week at the bottom of the Charles River? What was the least painful way to be murdered?

She shook her head. She couldn't go on thinking that way. Instead, she listed the reasons she still had to be thankful. They could have hurt her even more getting her into the car. Her stomach felt sore, but she didn't think she was seriously injured. Bruised up a little, but what would that matter if she got out of here alive?

Who were they? Hired men, perhaps? Had the Chinese government heard about her parents' clandestine missionary work? Was she some pawn now in an international conflict? She chided herself for watching too many spy shows with her dad. If only this were more like those. Then someone like James Bond would come and free her and kill her captors without breaking into a sweat or getting his tuxedo stained with blood.

"You hungry?" the man with the gruff voice asked. He

sounded a lot older than Dustin, but Kennedy hadn't gotten a good look at him before she was blindfolded.

The question startled Kennedy. What was this — a bed and breakfast for hostages? She was famished, and her mouth watered at the prospect of food, but she shook her head. *Tell them what you need*, she remembered her dad saying. But she didn't want to. She didn't want to be dependent on them. She didn't want to admit she would be here longer than a few minutes. She didn't want to acknowledge she was miles away from her dorm, maybe even in a different state, and nobody realized she was missing. How long before Reuben or Willow would get worried and start asking questions? A week? If these men had a copy of her phone and access to her email, couldn't they keep up the ruse of her disappearance indefinitely?

Maybe. But she wasn't going to accept that as a possibility. Right now, she was going to swallow down her heart, which kept threatening to leap out of her chest. She was going to ignore the rumbling in her stomach that felt as empty as the earth's upper atmosphere. She was going to think about pleasant things, like about the fact that God hadn't allowed them to force themselves on her, and she was going to plan a way to get out.

"Then we'll check on you in the morning," Dustin said.

Footsteps receded in the direction of the stairs. And then Kennedy — who had spent the last ten years in Yanji with its half a million residents, who now lived in a dorm with four hundred other students and shared her meals with nearly two thousand other college first-years — was left behind in stifling, deafening, soul-haunting solitude.

CHAPTER 13

She never knew what complete silence was until now. Her ears rang with it. Her mind waited for something — a shout, a yell, the horrifying pop of gunfire.

Nothing.

She reached up and touched her blindfold again, half expecting somebody to grab her wrist and stop her.

No one.

"Hello?" The sound of her own whisper sent goose bumps shivering up her spine. She thought of her high school psychology class, about how people could actually go crazy from sensory deprivation. Was that what this was?

She took off the blindfold with her free hand, but it was as dark as it had been. She couldn't see her own fingers and wished she had it back on again. Somehow knowing for certain she was in utter darkness was ten times more frightening than being blindfolded and only suspecting it.

Think. She had to think. Calm her mind and look at her

situation rationally. Like her dad would. She thought about the advice he gave the Secret Seminary students for handling solitary confinement. Develop a schedule. Keep a routine. Find some way to track the time. And pray.

Pray.

She thought about the refugees her parents had taken in back home. How many of them experienced darkness like this? What did they do? She thought of Hannah, the only girl who completed the whole Secret Seminary program. When Kennedy flew out to Massachusetts for college, Hannah was only a week or two away from returning to North Korea. Where was she now? Kennedy pictured Hannah's serene face. If Hannah were here, she would find a way to kneel in spite of the handcuff and spend the whole night in prayer — prayers for others probably, not even herself.

But Kennedy wasn't like that. She could never be as spiritually mature as Hannah or the other Secret Seminary students. She had never been asked to sneak into a closed nation where the penalty for evangelism was torture and death. She had never risked her life to share a Bible verse with someone else. At the All American Girls' High School, with all those preppy daughters of wealthy businessmen, Kennedy hadn't really shared her faith at all. That wasn't who she was. She liked watching action movies. She liked reading mysteries and shopping for clothes. She liked spending time with her friends. What was the crime in that? She still loved God, still believed in the Bible. She even had a vague notion of considering full- or part-time missions once she graduated from medical school in eight years. So why did it always feel like she wasn't doing enough?

She shivered from the cold and hugged her free arm around herself for extra warmth. Couldn't they have given her a blanket or something? Why had she been so stubborn and refused to tell them what she needed? She made a mental list of things to ask for when the men returned. Something hot to drink. A blanket. A pillow. She wondered how she was supposed to use the bathroom and thought again of how many others might have been chained all night to this very couch. Better ask for a sheet, too.

Her own materialism stared her accusingly in the face when she thought again about the members of her parents' Secret Seminary. What would they have requested? A Bible, no doubt. Well, she'd be surprised to find one of those here. This didn't seem like the kind of establishment the Gideons would keep stocked. This was definitely no hotel. If it was, she would order up room service, eat a big, fattening dinner, and lie down on a clean, puffy pillow ...

Why was she always so focused on her own needs, anyway? *Why can't you be more like Hannah?* She could almost hear her mother's accusing voice. Kennedy's mom spent hours each day with the Secret Seminary students, training, teaching, praying. Kennedy would come home from school and her mother would look shocked, surprised so much time had passed, surprised her own daughter was home and already interrupting their meeting.

Kennedy still spent time with her mom in Yanji, but it wasn't the same. It was always at night after her homework was done. Her mom would invite her to eat chocolate and watch old black and white movies in the bedroom. Kennedy wasn't part of the Secret Seminary, so nobody expected her to spend an hour on her knees praying. Nobody expected her to copy Scripture every day or memorize huge chunks of the Bible. Even when the North Korean students fasted, her mom still got up and fixed Kennedy breakfast each morning and gave her enough money to buy her lunch at school.

Why can't you be more like Hannah?

Kennedy gritted her teeth. She wasn't Hannah, and frankly, she didn't want to be. Why couldn't she be herself? She loved God. She prayed during the day and almost never ate a meal without thanking him for it first. So what was she missing? Why did it feel like she was never going to meet anybody's expectations?

When the first hot tear splashed onto Kennedy's arm, she tried to sniff all those negative emotions away. Sometimes she hated the Secret Seminary students, their courage, their commitment. She resented all the time her mom spent fussing over them, resented all the pride her mom lavished on them. Her mom was more impressed with the students for copying a book of the Bible than she was with Kennedy for being named valedictorian of her high school class. Her mom threw a lavish feast whenever a new refugee was baptized, and the whole household spent the day as if it were Christmas. What about when Kennedy got accepted into Harvard's early-admission medical school program fresh out of high school? She didn't get a feast or a new Bible or an impromptu worship service to thank God for her achievements. Instead, she got a few extra hugs, a whole backpack full of mystery novels for her summer reading, and a two-hundred-dollar gift certificate to her favorite online clothes store.

Even her dad babied her when he made her sit through the crisis training part of the Secret Seminary. The North Koreans would likely face interrogation at some point after returning home. He spoke about it as if it were a fact, and he gave them the practice and encouragement they'd need to endure. But even though he made Kennedy suffer through the exact same lectures and participate in the same role playing as the others, he didn't really think she could make it. That's why he made her watch those extra hours of self-defense videos before she left for college. With the Secret Seminary students, it was all about *turn the other cheek* and *love your enemies*. With Kennedy, it was *kick him in the groin* and *make a scene 'til someone comes to rescue you.*

Why? Because she wasn't cut from the same mold as the rest of them. She wasn't ever going to risk her life for Jesus. She wasn't ever going to be anything more than a Sunday-morning pew warmer. Her parents smothered her with gifts, let her go to dances and parties that no pastor's kid in the States would be allowed to attend, and only expected her to go to "church" in the den one morning a week. Maybe she was ready for more. Maybe her soul had been crying out for more, but her parents were too busy with their precious, anointed missionaries-in-training to notice.

And where was God? Where was he when she listened to her housemates in Yanji praying and asked him to make her as bold as they were? Where was he when she sat bored in church and begged God to fill her with the passion she saw in the refugees? When she was packing her things to move to Harvard, she prayed for Christian friends to meet her there. And God answered with Willow, the least likely student on campus to ever accept Christ, and Reuben, who claimed to be a Christian but refused to set foot in church.

Somewhere in the pit of her stomach, a howl threatened to rise. She kept it trapped in there for as long as she could. She clenched her jaw and tried to swallow it back down, but still it welled up from deep within her core, gathering strength and volume as it rose. It echoed against the walls, stinging her ears, chilling her marrow. She had never heard anything like it, not even in the movies. Almost animalistic, utterly hopeless, the sound of a spirit condemned to death.

By the time her tears ran dry, her ears still rang with its hollow echoes.

CHAPTER 14

"Wake up. Come on."

She didn't know what time it was, day or night. She didn't remember falling asleep on the musky couch. All she knew was she definitely wasn't rested.

She squinted in the beam from the flashlight, too disoriented to try to create a mental image of the room. She recognized Dustin as he stood by the couch and waved the flashlight in her eyes. "We need your help."

Kennedy had to find a toilet, and she wanted to wash some of the grime off her face. She was thirsty. He shone the beam at her, and she tried to raise both hands to her eyes before she remembered the cuff.

"You've got some medical training, right?" His voice was smaller now, rushed and anxious like a nervous fox.

"I'm pre-med. It's just my first year." Her voice was scratchy. How long had she been asleep? She tried to remember if Dustin was wearing the same flannel shirt as when he captured her, but she had been too busy getting beat up and thrown into a car to pay attention to the color and pattern.

"We need your help." His tone was still authoritative. Demanding. But Kennedy sensed an underlying desperation.

"I have to use the bathroom." She was pleased that her voice didn't give out on her. She sounded put together. Confident. If only she could feel that way, too.

"We don't have time for this," he mumbled to himself as he pulled a key out of his pocket. "All right, I'm going to show you where the bathroom is. You try something funny, I shoot you. Got it?" He swept up part of his shirt to show Kennedy the bottom of some kind of holster. Her spine stiffened at the sight.

"Yeah, I understand." She hoped he didn't feel her quiver when he unclasped the handcuff. She shook out her arm, relieved to be free of her restraint. Her legs were unstable when he led her to the bathroom, a big rusty setup which was more like a huge walk-in closet that happened to contain plumbing.

"Go on."

He stood outside, and she squatted over the rusty bowl so she didn't have to actually touch it. She tried not to think about the sound of her pee echoing in that great big room for everyone to hear. Well, if Dustin was an experienced kidnapper, he would be used to it.

Once she was done she walked to the sink, still unsteady. The water smelled like sulfur and was so cold it stung her hands. She decided not to wash her face, but she forced herself to gag down a little sip from her palms. The icy chill sent pangs of torment shooting to the roots of her teeth. She might not get anything else all day.

Or was it still night?

"You done?" He pounded on the door, and Kennedy looked around for one more second. Sometimes in the movies, there was a small ventilation window or a pipe to climb.

Nothing.

She stepped out of the bathroom.

"We've got someone you need to look at."

Dustin put his hand behind Kennedy's back. She could smell his BO and decided he must be wearing old clothes. Her odor probably wasn't much better. How long until she was able to take a shower? And if it was in that rotten-egg water, she'd probably pass anyway.

"She's having some sort of asthma attack or something," he told her. "Choking and crying up a storm."

Kennedy wondered who he was talking about. Was

this some sort of sex-slavery operation, then? Kennedy knew human trafficking was a huge problem in Asia, and her parents had even taken in a few girls who escaped from the hotel district in Yanji. But when her dad cited facts about forced prostitution in the US, she hadn't really paid attention. Something like that could never happen to her.

Could it?

"All right," Dustin called up the stairs. "Bring her down."

Kennedy heard the girl's wheezing, choking sobs even before she saw her in the poor light. She held her breath. What had they done to her?

"She won't hold still." Kennedy recognized the thick Boston accent of the driver. He came down the steps, struggling to carry the body that was kicking and flailing in his arms.

Kennedy's legs felt like they were supporting twice her body weight. There was no way the child was of age. Kennedy stepped forward, afraid the girl might thrash her way right down the staircase and break her neck.

"I need to talk to my dad!" She sucked in her breath in noisy, choppy spurts.

"She's been like this since we brought her in." The driver stepped into the light. He was older than Kennedy expected, built like a boxer and mostly bald. He glowered at Kennedy before he set the girl down on the couch. Kennedy cringed but didn't have time to think of all the germs and dust mites and rodents that probably made their home in its cushions.

The child covered her face with her hands and drew her knees to her chest. "I need my dad." Fitful sobs wracked her petite body.

Kennedy sensed the men's hopeful stares but forced them out of her mind. "It's all right," she whispered. "Everything is going to be ok."

The girl kept her face buried, and her shoulders heaved. "I don't want any more medicine."

Kennedy shot the two men a look, but they avoided her glare. "What's she talking about?"

"We have some pills. Doctor says it'll make her feel calmer. Anxiety medicine."

Kennedy didn't bother asking what sort of doctor would prescribe pills for a kidnapped child. "How long has she been here?" She forced an air of authority into her voice and stood up straight, stretching her spine tall.

"Half an hour. Maybe more."

"Have you had anything to eat?" she asked the child, who cringed when Kennedy touched her shoulder.

"She threw up on the way here," the bald man grumbled.

"Gonna stink up the car for weeks."

Kennedy reached out one more time. If she could only get her to look up ... What had these men already done to her? "Here, let me feel your forehead, ok?"

The girl glanced up, and Kennedy's breath caught somewhere in the middle of her throat. She would have recognized that face anywhere, even without the pearl earrings. Heart fluttering, she did what she could to keep her expression neutral. She gave what she hoped was a reassuring smile. The girl's brow was damp with sweat but didn't feel feverish. Her collarbone strained with each irregular breath.

"I need more light," Kennedy told them.

"Plug in the lamp," the driver told his partner and jerked his flashlight toward the wall. Pain pulsed to the back of Kennedy's head as soon as Dustin switched the light on. She blinked. The girl's lips were outlined in grayish blue, and her mouth hung open in an inaudible little gasp. Her chest moved as if trying to inhale, but no air went in.

How long had they said this had been going on? "Is there a shower here?" Kennedy heard the worried strain in her own voice. "Something that could make some steam?"

"What good's that gonna do?" the driver demanded.

"It can open up all the airways. Help her breathe more

evenly." Kennedy bit her lip while the men looked at each other.

"We don't got a water heater."

The girl's shoulders shuddered as her body attempted another jerky inhale. They had to do something.

"Is there a way to boil some water?"

The bald man shook his head, and the girl let out a long wheezy sob.

Kennedy reached for her clammy hand. "You can go buy a face steamer. They have them at just about any drugstore." Her heart was thudding loudly in her chest. Would they do that much? Would these kidnappers have the decency to help a little girl from suffocating on their mildewy couch?

"Get over here." The balding one gestured with his head, and both men moved to the base of the stairs and conferred in low whispers.

Keeping one eye on the pair, Kennedy stroked the girl's hair and whispered out of the corner of her mouth, "Is your name Jodie?"

The child bent over. The wheezing sound from her lungs made Kennedy vicariously faint-headed.

"Jodie Abernathy?" Kennedy asked again.

A single tear splashed into the girl's lap as her lungs forced a noisy gulp of air. Her breath was as choppy as a windy lake in the fall, but she didn't respond.

Kennedy wanted to hug her, to make her body into a shield that would ward off panic and terror. "It's all right to be scared," she whispered before Dustin stepped back into the light.

"Face steamer, it's called?"

Kennedy nodded. She didn't trust her voice. He returned to his partner.

"I think we've talked before." Kennedy kept her tone soft. She was afraid that saying too much might trigger another wave of panic. "Did you make a phone call from St. Margaret's on Sunday?"

Jodie sniffed and gave an almost imperceptible nod. A small jolt sent Kennedy's heart galloping one more time.

She had found Rose.

CHAPTER 15

"Do you know these men?" Kennedy had a hundred questions and probably less than a minute to ask them all.

"No." Jodie sniffed again.

Kennedy didn't realize she had been holding her breath until she let out the next torrent of queries. "Are you hurt? Did they make you do anything you didn't want to do? Did they ... did they force ..." She couldn't finish the sentence.

Jodie shook her head, and relief radiated out of Kennedy's core all the way to her fingertips, warming her whole body.

The older man stomped up the stairs. "Don't let them out of your sight," he called down.

Dustin didn't look over at Kennedy and Jodie. "I know."

Kennedy watched the older one pass out of view. Was he going to get the steamer, then? Jodie's breathing was a little quieter, and Kennedy hoped he wouldn't change his mind. She held Jodie for several minutes, keeping her eye on Dustin, who stood at the bottom of the stairs scowling.

She ran her hands through the girl's hair. "How are you feeling?"

"Thirsty." Jodie was quieter now and hiccupping.

Kennedy caught Dustin's eye. "I think she might be dehydrated."

He stared at Jodie for a few silent seconds. "I have some water bottles upstairs," he finally mumbled. "I'll get one when Vinny gets back."

Kennedy sucked in her breath. "What about the bathroom?" She tried not to wince when she remembered the taste of the sulfur water from the tap. "Could she get a drink there?"

"Whatever," Dustin huffed.

"Do you think you can stand by yourself?" Kennedy asked. She needed a chance to talk to Jodie privately. She stood up and then paused. Would Dustin come over and stop her? After a moment of waiting to see if he would protest, she helped Jodie to her feet, and they shuffled together to the bathroom.

"Do you have any idea who these guys are?" Kennedy whispered once she shut the door. "Even a guess?"

"Uh-uh." Jodie's wide eyes blinked in the flickering light from the bulb.

"Are you having a little easier time breathing, at least?"

Jodie scrunched up her face. "I just ..." Her shoulders heaved with another choppy breath. "I just want my dad."

Kennedy didn't want to think about Wayne Abernathy and what his role might be in this whole scenario. "I'm sure you do." She should try to get more information. She should keep on asking Jodie questions until eventually the pieces fell into place. But she couldn't. Not when the little indent of Jodie's neck quivered each time she tried to inhale.

Kennedy rubbed Jodie's back. "Can you try to drink a little water?"

"I want my dad." Jodie took a noisy gasp in, and Kennedy paused to see if she would start hyperventilating again.

What could she say to keep her from panicking? There had to be some sort of encouragement, some sort of comfort she could offer. "You go to St. Margaret's, right?"

Jodie nodded.

"Well, you know how Pastor Carl and your Sunday school teachers are always talking about giving your worries to God?"

"Yeah." The response was appropriate, but Jodie didn't sound at all convinced.

"It's a good idea. He's here with us, you know." Kennedy wondered how long they had before Dustin ran out of patience. "The Lord's watching us right now. And I think he's going to help us get out of this." There was no real faith behind that last statement, but Jodie's body relaxed a little. "Do you know any Bible verses?" Kennedy asked.

"Psalm 23." Jodie wrinkled her nose when Kennedy turned on the water.

"Psalm 23's a good one." Kennedy did her best to infuse her tone with encouragement while Jodie cupped her hands and took a small drink. "Do you want to say it together?"

Jodie took a slow breath in and kept her face scrunched up after she swallowed the water from the sink. "*The Lord is my ...*"

"That's enough."

Jodie and Kennedy both jumped when Dustin banged on the door. Kennedy wasn't about to see how far his generosity ran. She stepped out of the bathroom, grateful to see he wasn't wielding his gun. "We were just finishing up."

He grunted in response.

Kennedy led Jodie back and didn't flinch when Dustin cuffed her left hand back to the metal hook that stuck out of the wall. He frowned at Jodie, and Kennedy wondered if he would cuff her, too. Would that start off another panic attack?

Instead, he went back to the wall by the stairs and spent the rest of the time before Vinny returned fiddling at the tool table and glancing at the stairs every so often. Kennedy's mind spun in multiple directions at once. What she really needed was more time to talk to Jodie about Wayne Abernathy, about his campaign, about any enemies he had made. She had read enough political thrillers and watched enough action movies with her dad to know a desperate candidate could do about anything, even stoop to kidnapping. But why had they grabbed Kennedy, too?

Her brain raced ahead, whizzing and gyrating. Puzzle pieces arranged themselves up in perfect rows faster than she had time to connect them all. A hot shower, that's what she needed. A hot shower, some tea, and a notebook to jot down all her questions. Right now, she felt she could fill a whole composition book with them.

"There weren't no face steamers there." The voice pierced the silence and made Kennedy wince. Vinny glowered down from the top of the stairs, his face set into an imposing scowl.

Jodie's tiny body quivered as he stomped down the stairs. Every step seemed to take twice as long as it should.

"It will be all right," Kennedy whispered, wondering if Jodie could guess how terrified she was, too.

At the couch, Vinny crossed his arms and scrutinized Jodie. "She looks better." Kennedy couldn't tell if Vinny was making a simple observation or if he had decided Jodie's condition was no longer serious.

Kennedy stared past his ear and clenched her sweat-drenched palms. "Well, that's the funny thing with asthma. Sometimes it gets better all by itself, and sometimes it gets so bad you'll end up in the hospital." She wondered if her roommate Willow would be impressed with her improv performance. Whatever happened, she couldn't let them take Jodie back upstairs alone. They had to stay together. *Are you listening, God?*

Vinny's phone rang, and he stomped off to the far wall to answer it. Jodie breathed in deeply. "I don't really have asthma."

"I didn't think so." Kennedy spoke out of the corner of her mouth. "But if they think you need more help, like you're sick or something, they might let us stay together longer."

Jodie nodded and her hand crept toward Kennedy's.

"They're probably not going to hurt us." Kennedy hoped her voice sounded more confident than she felt.

When Vinny got off the phone, he jerked his head, and

Dustin joined him for another conference out of earshot.

Kennedy waited a minute until the men were absorbed in their hushed whispers. "When did you get here?"

"Just this morning." Jodie wiped her nose with her palm. Kennedy thought she had made a mistake in asking. Would Jodie start hyperventilating again? But she needed answers. She had to strain her ears to hear what Jodie said next. "I went to my uncle Anthony's to babysit. He was going to be out late, so he wanted me to stay overnight."

Revulsion bubbled up Kennedy's throat. "Do you spend the night with your uncle very often?"

Jodie shrugged. "Only since my aunt died. Sometimes he's out late and needs help with Charlie."

Kennedy focused her gaze straight ahead and waited until the swell of suspicion and disgust settled back down in her gut. "So does your uncle know you're here?"

"No." Jodie's eyes grew wide. "They came about an hour after he left. And I don't know what they did to Charlie." Jodie buried her face in her hands. "They might have hurt him."

Kennedy couldn't imagine being a thirteen-year-old and shouldering such a weighty responsibility. "Whatever happened isn't your fault." She prayed the Lord would give her the right words to say so Jodie could truly believe it.

"But he's so little. He just turned one last month." Jodie's voice hardly lifted over a whisper but was laden with terror. "He must have been so scared, and I wasn't there ..."

"You don't know if anything happened to Charlie, right? I mean, maybe he's just fine and safe at home."

Jodie shook her head. "But then he's all by himself. He doesn't even walk yet." A little sob forced its way out her throat.

"Well, maybe your uncle stopped by to check on you. Or maybe he called and you weren't there, so he went home. We don't know." Kennedy's whole torso was quivering again, but she hoped Jodie wouldn't notice. Her mind was spinning. If Jodie's uncle reported her missing, that would mean people were looking for them. They might get rescued, after all. She didn't want to raise Jodie's hopes, so she kept the thought secret and suggested, "Why don't you say a prayer for Charlie?"

Jodie dried her cheeks. "Do you really think that would help?"

Kennedy swallowed down her doubts. "I'm sure of it."

"You want me to pray right here?"

Kennedy glanced at Dustin behind the workbench and Vinny on the phone. "Don't worry. They're not paying attention."

"All right." Jodie collected her breath. "God, please help Charlie not to be really scared. And we hope he's at home right now and that someone's there playing with him so he stays happy. Amen."

Kennedy wondered at the simplicity of this prayer compared to the hour-long discourses she was used to hearing back in Yanji. Somehow, she figured these few sentences meant as much to the Lord as a whole treatise would have. Kennedy was about to add a prayer of her own when Vinny slammed the phone back into his pocket and stomped toward the couch, fists clenched, eyes glaring. She felt Jodie's whole body go rigid next to her.

"All right. Your little coughing fit's over. Time to take your medicine."

CHAPTER 16

Jodie shut her eyes and shook her head weakly. "I don't like those pills."

"I didn't ask if you liked them," Vinny snapped back. "Open your mouth."

"How many are there?" Kennedy asked when she saw more than one in his hand.

"Four. She's gotta take them all at once."

Kennedy had never heard of a dose that large for anxiety meds, especially for a child as small as Jodie.

"I don't like them," Jodie moaned again.

Even though her hand was still cuffed to the metal ring, Kennedy tried to position herself a little in front of Jodie. It wasn't hard since Jodie scurried behind her, scrunching herself up in between Kennedy and the couch cushion.

"Do you take these regularly?" Kennedy asked. If these men expected her to care for Jodie when she was hyperventilating, she was going to keep up her air of medical superiority at all costs. All the clues from the past few days — the phone, the uncle, the clinic, the kidnapping — played out in flashes in Kennedy's mind. They were racing to set themselves in logical order, and the closer she got to the full picture, the more dread grew and made its home in the center of her gut.

"My uncle gave me one after church." Jodie was curled up in the couch, and Kennedy could hardly hear her. "It made me throw up."

"What medicine is it?" Kennedy tried not to cower in front of Vinny, whose scowl radiated both impatience and contempt.

"I already told you. It's for anxiety."

Kennedy saw the hateful gleam in his eye. He was probably armed like his partner. She felt as nervous as she had as a child when she went ice skating on a frozen pond, trying hard to balance, all the while expecting the ice to crack beneath her at the slightest shift in weight.

"Can she take them after she eats something?" Kennedy tried to speak confidently without being too abrasive, either. "That might help with the nausea."

Time. Kennedy needed more time. Time to think. Time to sort out all her thoughts. And a snack for both of them wouldn't hurt, either.

Vinny's expression may as well have been etched in granite. "She takes them now."

"I don't need them anymore. I don't feel anxious at all." Jodie's voice was a pitiful little yelp squeaking out from behind the couch cushion.

"Your uncle Anthony says you need them."

At the mention of Jodie's uncle, Kennedy felt the floor had been slipped out from under her, like those inertia magic tricks when the magician pulls off the tablecloth.

"My uncle?" the child squeaked. "He knows I'm here?"

"We've been in contact," Vinny answered gruffly. "And he wants you to take your pills."

Kennedy scratched her cheek. Jodie's uncle. So he was involved. Thoughts collided against each other in Kennedy's brain as the pieces of the puzzle zoomed into place. The uncle. The same man who had overheard Jodie's phone call to the hotline phone. The same man who wanted her to get rid of her baby. Kennedy eyed the white tablets again as warning alarms screeched and squealed between her temples, unleashing a torrent of adrenaline and pure rage. How far along had Jodie said she was in the pregnancy? Five months?

Kennedy kept herself positioned squarely between Jodie and Vinny. "She can't take those."

He reached out to push her out of the way, but Kennedy slapped the pills out of his hand. He grabbed a fistful of her hair and jerked her head to the side. Before he picked up the fallen tablets, she tried to sweep them away with her foot.

"Wait! They're not safe this late." Kennedy clawed at his forearms as Vinny pinched Jodie's cheeks together.

He forced her mouth open. "Take them."

Kennedy winced as the handcuff cut against her wrist, but she hardly registered the pain. Anger, fright, and horror all mingled together, poisoning her blood, tinting her vision. She tried to knock Vinny's hand out of the way. Dustin appeared behind the couch and forced Jodie's mouth open once more.

"She can't take them." Kennedy reached with her free hand to scratch at Dustin, but he only strengthened his grip on Jodie's jaw. Gurgling noise came from the back of Jodie's throat. Dustin was holding her head so tight the veins in his forearms popped up.

Vinny loomed over them both, towering over Jodie with the pills in his hand. Kennedy tried to kick him away. He clenched his fist, and then pain splintered across Kennedy's temple. Her head jerked back right before Vinny punched her again in the gut. For a moment, she was paralyzed. She couldn't see. She couldn't breathe. She sensed the commotion around her but couldn't process any of it.

"Hold her head steady," Vinny growled.

"I'm trying."

Kennedy could hear the strain in both men's voices. Jodie was still struggling, but what chance did a thirteen-year-old girl have against two armed men? A toxic, murderous fury boiled over from somewhere deep within Kennedy's core, and she kicked Vinny in the shin. He cursed and lunged at her. She let out a roar and kicked him once more, this time in the groin. He dropped the pills and fell on the couch.

Jodie cried out once when he landed with his elbow on her midsection.

The room fell silent except for Jodie's tiny sobs. With her toe Kennedy nudged one of the pills under the couch and snuck her other foot over two more. She couldn't find the fourth. The pained grimace on Vinny's face morphed into a mask of rage, and hatred dripped from his entire countenance.

"You little ..."

Kennedy tried not to shrink back. *God, you have to get us out of here.* Her heart was thudding violently, pounding as if its one purpose in life was to beat its way out of her

159

chest.

"Where are the pills?" Vinny spoke each word slowly, allowing his malicious venom to lace every syllable.

Kennedy tried crushing the two pills underfoot with her shoe, but they were too durable.

"She kicked one under the couch," Dustin declared.

"Stand up." Vinny's voice was now eerily controlled.

Kennedy got off the couch but had to lean over Jodie since one of her wrists was still cuffed. Her face was a few inches away from Jodie, who cried softly into her hands. *I'm sorry*, she wished she could say. *I'm so sorry.*

"Pick up your foot."

Kennedy shut her eyes. *Forgive them Lord, for they know not what they do.* Only that didn't apply here. Vinny knew exactly what he was doing. Was he really that deranged? Did he hold such little regard for Jodie and her safety? For the life she carried? Didn't he know what those pills would do? How could he work for someone related to Wayne Abernathy, whose name was synonymous with the pro-life movement in Massachusetts? So was Jodie's father involved, too? A dozen potential scenarios, each more troublesome than the previous, whirled their way around Kennedy's mind in a convoluted, dizzying blur.

She let out her breath, defeated, and took her foot off

the two pills she had tried to hide. *I'm sorry, Jodie. I'm so sorry.*

Vinny kept his eyes on Kennedy. She could feel the heat from his stare boring into her forehead before he jerked his head at Dustin. "Pick them up."

Dustin came around to the front of the couch.

"Check and see if you can find the others," Vinny ordered.

A lone, silent tear slipped down Kennedy's cheek. She couldn't bring herself to look at anyone. What was the point of reaching the top of her high school class if she had to stand by and do nothing while a poor, victimized child was forced to swallow abortion pills that would kill her child and ravage her body? What was the point of studying in college until her eyes burned if she couldn't help a little girl or the baby she was too young to carry? She forced herself to look at Jodie's heaving shoulders. What was the point of worshipping a God who wouldn't lift his finger to rescue these precious souls?

The thought was blasphemous, but for the moment she didn't care. How could Christians understand the evil that flourishes in this world and still walk around with their happy smiles and talk about God's blessings? How could Christians confront such brutal, beastly violence and then fold their hands and thank God for his providence? She bit her lip to keep it from trembling and guessed what her dad would say:

And we know that all things work together for the good of those who love God. Well, Kennedy loved God. She had given up her rights to a "normal" American childhood and watched her parents start their Secret Seminary overseas. She had sacrificed time she didn't have to volunteer at the pregnancy center, and now she might never go back to her dorm. She might never talk to her mom or dad again. Another tear leaked down her face.

She didn't fight when Dustin bent down inches from her and picked up the pills. She didn't stomp on his fingers or try to kick his nose when he swept his hand under the couch and found the two others. Up until now, she thought the phrase *pick your battles* referred to minor compromises to help you get along with your family members or roommates. She hadn't ever stopped to think that sometimes you have to give up the most worthy of battles, the battles that deserve to be fought, the battles that hold life and dignity and innocence captive.

Dustin stood up. Vinny reached his hand out. "You will take these. Now." He fixed his gaze on Kennedy. "And you won't get in the way."

Kennedy didn't have the strength to cringe.

Jodie took the pills in her hand. In her eyes, Kennedy saw

the same resigned sadness that squeezed and wrung her own soul as if it were a soppy-wet rag. "Can I have some water?" Jodie's voice was quiet, but it didn't tremble.

Vinny glared for a second longer and then strode to the tool table and grabbed some sort of thermos. As he stomped to the bathroom, Kennedy stared down at the floor.

"Here," Vinny grumbled when he returned, splashing water when he thrust the cup in front of Jodie.

She raised her eyebrows once at Kennedy. That single, trusting, hopeful look stabbed Kennedy's heart like a thousand guilt-laced arrows. She blinked back her tears and gave the child a nod. *Forgive them, Father, for they know not what they do ...*

Jodie uncurled her legs out from beneath her. She put her feet on the floor and reached for the cup. Kennedy's throat threatened to collapse on itself. Part of her wanted to force her eyes away. The other part wanted to brand each small detail into the recesses of her memory. Maybe God could forgive Jodie's uncle and kidnappers for what they were forcing her to do, but Kennedy never could. She steeled up her heart, fortified its chambers with walls of cool, calculating wrath, and wondered if she had ever really understood the phrase *righteous indignation* until this exact moment.

The thermos trembled in Jodie's hand. Kennedy sucked in her breath, steeling herself.

The tin cup clattered on the floor. The water splashed out and sprayed Kennedy's leg. The pills made the smallest of thuds when they hit the ground. Jodie yelped and jumped to her feet. Everyone stared at the front of her pants.

She was covered in blood.

CHAPTER 17

Kennedy forced a deep breath into her lungs even though her diaphragm threatened to spasm. Her head felt light. Whatever energy she still had left seeped out of her body and dissipated into the air.

Ignoring the spinning in the center of her brain, Kennedy balled her hands into fists and glowered at Vinny. "What did you do?" She recognized a hint of hysteria sneaking into her tone but couldn't control it.

Vinny was still frozen, his angry scowl cemented in place. Kennedy couldn't stomach the sight of him, but she met his glare with open hostility. That was another difference between her and the Secret Seminary students. Hannah and the others might be able to love their enemies. But if she ever broke free, Kennedy wouldn't sleep until Vinny was either dead or rotting away in a general population prison, where she hoped the inmates' sense of vigilante justice would only prolong his suffering.

She narrowed her eyes and thought about the big pit bull terrier that lived next door when she was a little girl. *If he meets your stare, don't be the first to look away.* She didn't know how long her face-off with Vinny would have lasted because after a few seconds, Jodie sunk back on the couch with a moan. "My stomach hurts."

At the sound of the tiny whine, Kennedy and Vinny both turned to the couch. Jodie's hands were clasped around her midsection. The wet spot of blood on her lap was even larger than before.

Contempt heated up Kennedy's whole body. *Stay calm,* she told herself. *Remember, you're still their prisoner.* She took another breath and swallowed down her disgust. "Would it be all right if I took her into the bathroom?" She remembered the men credited her with some degree of medical knowledge. "She might have gotten injured when you fell on her."

Vinny looked aside. "You have five minutes," he growled without changing his facial expression. A jerk of the head sent Dustin fumbling with the handcuff key.

When Kennedy was free, she put her arm around Jodie. "Do you think you can walk?"

Jodie grimaced. "It hurts."

"I'm going to stand up first, and then I'll help you, ok?"

Kennedy blinked over her dry contacts. She pulled Jodie to her feet, and the child let out another whimper.

Kennedy was so weak she could hardly stand up straight, but she managed to shuffle toward the bathroom, half dragging, half carrying Jodie. A few steps away from the door, she lost her footing and nearly stumbled. She clenched her jaw shut to ward off the frustrated scream that threatened to jump from her throat. Why were they here? Why was any of this happening? And if Jodie needed real medical intervention, what in the world could Kennedy do about it in this cold, musty basement?

Please God, we need a miracle. We need to be rescued. Kennedy grew up learning God had amazing plans for her. When she heard stories of believers who went through incredible suffering or persecution, she figured that they were the unlucky ones like Job, but in the end they too would have their reward. She assumed her own life would continue on as always, paved with blessings, filled with abundance, sheltered from tragedy, free from fear. Could it really be that last week the biggest stress was the calculus test she was now missing?

She thought about *Crime and Punishment.* What would Dostoevsky say about her situation? Probably not much. Her case was one more petty injustice in a world teeming with suffering and evil. Kennedy had never felt so insignificant, so invisible. She bit her lip, repositioned her weight, and helped Jodie take the last few steps to the bathroom.

"Five minutes," Vinny repeated behind them.

Kennedy shut the door. A whole day, a whole week of prayer wouldn't have prepared her for any of this. What was she supposed to do now? How was she supposed to help Jodie? Kennedy wanted to find the man who came up with the catchphrase, *God wouldn't give you more than you could handle*, and laugh in his face. Or maybe shake him by the shoulders.

Jodie dropped to the ground when the door closed. Kennedy cringed when she thought about how many bacterial colonies were thriving down there. "Do you want to sit on the toilet or something?" Not that it was any cleaner.

Jodie stared into her lap. "I'm bleeding."

"I know, sweetie. I think something ..." Kennedy stopped herself. She didn't know what was going on. Had Vinny hurt her when he fell on her? Or was it something else? "I think we just need to see about getting you cleaned up. Can you come up here?" She patted the back of the toilet bowl and immediately wished she hadn't.

Jodie glanced at the toilet the same way Kennedy might have stared at the Demilitarized Zone between North and South Korea after someone told her she should race across it. But she couldn't leave the girl on the floor, could she?

"I think I wet my pants," Jodie finally confessed.

"Don't worry about that. Let's get you up here, and we'll see if we can clean you up some." Kennedy doubted the men had a change of clothes here.

After she helped Jodie onto the toilet, she opened the bathroom door a small crack. Dustin was standing outside, but his gun was still concealed. "She's bleeding pretty heavy." Kennedy's face warmed with humiliation, and she kept her eyes low. She didn't want Jodie to think she was embarrassed, and she forced her voice to sound natural. "Can we have some pads?"

Dustin looked over his shoulder at Vinny, who was tinkering again at the work table. "What do they need?" he grumbled.

"Pads." A small hint of pink dusted the tips of Dustin's ears.

"Pads what?" Vinny yelled back. "Pads of paper?"

Dustin looked once to Kennedy before answering, "No, pads. You know. For girls." The last two words came out reluctantly.

Vinny slammed his wrench onto the table. "You go get them, then."

Dustin didn't object. Kennedy wouldn't have either, not

when Vinny used that tone of voice. Dustin went up the stairs without saying anything else. Kennedy reminded herself to try to gauge how long he was gone. That might give her some clue how far away they were from real people and real stores. She wasn't sure exactly how that knowledge could help her, though. What they needed was a real SWAT team with real tactical gear. She thought about Dustin's gun and wondered what other weapons the men had stashed around here.

With Dustin gone and Vinny tied up with whatever project he was working on, Kennedy and Jodie could have a little privacy. She shut the door the rest of the way. Jodie was still clutching her stomach, and in the artificial light from the bulb hanging overhead, her skin looked a strange shade of grayish green.

"This hasn't been a very good day for you, has it?" Kennedy was half joking and didn't really expect a response. She didn't know what else to say. She had dozens of questions, but any one of them would remind Jodie of their awful situation. Another panic fit was the last thing either of them needed. "How's your stomach feel?"

"A little better, I guess." Jodie offered Kennedy a weak smile. "Thanks for being here."

Kennedy forced herself to chuckle. "I could say the same to you, too. I definitely wouldn't want to be alone right now." She didn't know how late it was but figured it was some time Tuesday afternoon. At school, she would either be cramming for calculus or taking that test. It seemed silly now, all the time and energy Kennedy had spent worrying and stressing over her GPA.

"So, you know what you were saying before?" Jodie began. "About God being with you?"

Kennedy had never had a serious conversation — or a conversation of any kind — in a bathroom with someone who was bleeding on the toilet, but what was it she had told Reuben a few days ago? *First time for everything.* She waited for Jodie to continue.

"Well, I was wondering. Do you think, I mean, do you think he's with you even when you do something bad ... like have an abortion or something?"

The question hit Kennedy like a kick to the gut. So did Jodie know the truth about the pills? "Sweetie, what your uncle tried to make you do ... that wasn't your fault, you know. You didn't have any control over that."

"Yeah, but ..." Jodie bit her lip. "I actually told him I would. Have an abortion, I mean."

Kennedy hoped if she ever got out of here that God would keep Jodie's uncle in another country, preferably on another continent. Kennedy didn't want the guilt of murder on her hands, but she sure felt capable of it every time she thought about Anthony Abernathy. She couldn't let Jodie know though, so she nodded and asked, "When did you tell him that?"

"Well, he said that if I let him take me to this clinic after church that he'd ... well, he's going to France this Christmas. And he said he'd want me to go and be Charlie's nanny while he's there, and I've never been to another country, so ..."

Jodie nodded and kept her gaze on the grimy floor.

"And so after church my parents thought I was just going to play with Charlie for a few hours, but we took him to his grandma's and went to the clinic instead."

"What happened there?" Kennedy felt like she was reading an overly-violent scene in a novel. Her initial reaction was to skim past it all, but her brain forced her to pay attention to each word so she didn't miss anything. Instead of speeding up past the gruesomeness of it all, her mind slowed down as if it wanted to absorb the horror in small bits at a time.

"Well, I started crying. It was hard to breathe."

"Kind of like this morning?" Kennedy asked.

Jodie nodded.

"That's a panic attack, sweetie. It feels really scary, but

you've just gone through a whole lot. It's your body's way of showing you it's frightened." Kennedy realized then she didn't know half of what Jodie had endured. Almost all of it was still conjecture. "It's a natural reaction for someone who's gone through as much as you have."

"I told them I didn't want to do it." Jodie's voice trembled a little. "I was screaming. My uncle had to hold me down." She hung her head.

Kennedy's skin tingled with rage. "Did he force you?" She had been horrified by the video her dad made her watch once about abortions, and that was when she was a senior in high school. She couldn't imagine what it would be like for a thirteen-year-old girl to have to suffer first-hand through something so traumatic.

Jodie shook her head. "No, he would never do that."

Apparently Jodie had a higher opinion of her uncle than he deserved, but Kennedy kept the thought to herself.

"He went outside for a minute to talk to the nurse. And then he came back and gave me a pill. He said I had a case of nerves — that's what the crying was about — and that I should take it to feel calmer. But it didn't help. I started throwing up really bad. Not just like the morning sickness, either."

Kennedy still couldn't get used to the idea that she was

standing in a bathroom talking to a junior-higher about things like morning sickness and abortion clinics.

"Is that why you didn't want to take the pills the guys out there gave you?"

Jodie sniffed and nodded. "I've just been feeling so bad lately. I went to this forum online, and it said morning sickness usually goes away after the first twelve weeks, but it didn't."

"Well, I can see why you maybe thought that having an abortion was the only option." Kennedy hated saying the words. What kind of life had Jodie led to think there wasn't anything else she could do? On the other hand, given her age, given her family situation and the media hype over the upcoming election, would carrying the child have been any less horrific and traumatizing? "I'm proud of you, though, for changing your mind. That must have taken a lot of courage."

Jodie sniffed. "I didn't do it for the baby or anything, you know."

"What do you mean?"

"The nurse said they'd have to do an ultrasound. See how old the baby was. And I ..." Jodie sniffed again and turned her face. "I didn't want my uncle to know. He only thinks I'm six weeks." Jodie's voice was so quiet Kennedy had to lean down toward her a little.

"Why did you tell him that?"

"I didn't want to get Samir in trouble. He was ... he ... we were good friends. But our parents didn't like us spending time together." She kept her eyes to the ground. "Last summer his family sent him to a boys' home in Vermont. I think they just wanted to make sure we couldn't be around each other. I haven't talked to him since then."

"I'm sorry." Was there anything else for Kennedy to say? None of this made any sense.

Jodie looked up shyly. "If my uncle knew I got pregnant that long ago, he would have thought the baby was ... Well, you know. And he'd be mad at Samir. Really mad."

Something about Jodie's tone didn't fit with the rest of the story. Of course, it was unnaturally bizarre talking to someone so young about boyfriends and abortions and pregnancies, but was that all, or was there more to it? Was Jodie telling her everything?

Jodie sucked in her breath. "That's why I said I didn't want the abortion after all. I didn't want the nurse to do the ultrasound and tell my uncle how old the baby really was."

Kennedy tried to swallow. Why did she live in a world where girls so young could get pregnant in the first place? "We all make mistakes," she stammered. She thought about her junior-high crushes. Sure, they felt like real love, but she

175

couldn't imagine going to bed with someone at that age. "I know if you're really sorry for what you and Samir did ..."

Jodie scrunched up her face. "But we never did anything."

Kennedy felt like she had when she first moved to Yanji, trying to understand the new language, knowing she had missed something important but unable to figure out what. "So Samir's not the dad?" She felt like a bigger dolt than she had when everyone in her calculus study group figured out how to derive differential equations before she did.

Jodie shook her head. "No. We never even kissed. I didn't want Uncle Anthony to think Samir got me pregnant. But he and I ..." She lowered her eyes again. "We didn't do anything like that. He's not even a Christian. We liked each other a lot, but neither of our parents would allow it. Besides, we both knew it would be wrong."

So she lied to her uncle to protect a boy who couldn't possibly be the baby's father?

"Guess you're surprised." Jodie let out a mirthless laugh that could have come from somebody much older. "With my dad being so pro-life and all."

Kennedy thought her next words out very carefully and kept her gaze fixed to discern Jodie's reaction to each syllable. "Well, if Samir's not the one who got you pregnant

..." she began tentatively.

Jodie turned her head and sat up a little straighter. Did she know what was coming?

Kennedy's hands started to sweat, and she wiped them on the sides of her pants. "You don't have to tell me anything if you don't want to, but I think it would be helpful if I knew." Her mouth felt suddenly very dry. She swallowed before she began again. "Sometimes adults don't know the right way to treat their daughters or their nieces, and they ... What I'm trying to ask you is if your dad or maybe your uncle is the one who ..."

There was a banging on the door. "Times up."

Jodie let out a loud, choppy sigh. Kennedy was just as ready to end the conversation there, at least for now. She was sure that hadn't been a full five minutes, but she was in no position to argue. She eyed Jodie's stained clothes. "What you want to do about your pants?"

Vinny pounded on the door again. If he grew too impatient, nothing could stop him from coming in before Jodie was dressed.

"We're getting ready right now," she called out in the least hostile tone she could stomach. She frowned at Jodie. "I'm really sorry, but I think the only choice is to put your old clothes back on for now. At least when the other guy gets back with some pads ..." She let her voice trail off and wondered for the hundredth time that day how she had gone from a volunteer weekend receptionist to a hostage in this huge, impenetrable cell.

Jodie could move more easily now, and she only needed a little help to keep her balance as she dressed. Kennedy helped her roll up some toilet paper to serve as a makeshift pad and tried not to cringe when Jodie put on the bloodstained things. It was better than wearing nothing at all.

A second before Jodie finished pulling her pants up, Vinny barged into the bathroom. "I said time's up," he growled. Kennedy avoided his eyes and linked her elbow in Jodie's. They walked back to the couch, and Vinny's phone rang. Kennedy hoped she could continue her awkward conversation with Jodie, but he just looked at his screen, swore, and jammed the phone back into his pocket.

"It's cold." Jodie sat and hugged her arms around herself. She was shivering. For a minute, Kennedy thought about asking Vinny for a blanket, but she decided to wait. Maybe Dustin would be in a more agreeable mood when he came back with the pads. It seemed nearly impossible for their situation to improve in any way, but she could always hope.

CHAPTER 18

Jodie curled herself up in a little ball on the couch, resting her head on Kennedy's lap. Kennedy stroked her hair and remembered cuddling with her mom like that in front of the TV when she was a little girl. But she couldn't think about her mom right now. She couldn't think about her friends she left back on campus or the homework assignments she was missing. She only had the mental stamina to worry about Jodie.

Thankfully, Jodie didn't seem to be in as much pain. The cold was her only real complaint. While they rested and waited for Dustin to return, Kennedy inventoried all the information she had stored up over the past few days. Dustin and Vinny were working for Jodie's uncle, and he was the one who wanted Jodie to take those abortion pills. Did he know what they would do to her body? If he knew how far along Jodie really was, would he still make her take them? Was he willing to risk his niece's life simply to keep the family from scandal? Was this whole act a desperate struggle to save his brother's campaign? Or would things be different if he knew the real age of Jodie's baby?

Since Jodie's friend Samir wasn't the dad, who got her pregnant in the first place? It was possible Jodie was lying, but Kennedy couldn't picture someone as quiet and demure as Jodie sneaking around with boys behind her parents' backs. Jodie had made a comment on the phone about her dad. What was it that she had said? At the time, Kennedy would have guessed she was being abused by her own father. She had only talked with Senator Abernathy for a few minutes and came back with conflicting impressions. On the one hand, he seemed as plastic and insincere as she would expect from any other politician. Even if he wasn't directly responsible for abusing his daughter, wouldn't he be close enough to his brother to know what a dangerous influence he was? But then Kennedy thought about the way he talked about his work in the pro-life movement, the concern he showed not only for the unborn babies but for the moms who carried them. Could he really be so two-faced to abuse his own daughter or stand by while her uncle tried to bribe her into having an abortion? Was there any possibility he was completely innocent in the matter?

Whether or not Jodie's dad was involved, her uncle

definitely was. She had a low enough opinion of Anthony Abernathy to immediately suspect him. Anyone capable of kidnapping and forced abortions was capable of child abuse, right? But why did he go through the trouble to have Kennedy kidnapped, too? Even if he knew about Jodie's call to the pregnancy center, he didn't have any way to link that conversation back to Kennedy. Unless …

The sound of smashed glass crunching on the pavement echoed in Kennedy's mind. The sight of the graffiti, the heaviness in the air when Carl and Sandy surveyed the destruction and vandalism of their new ministry building. Was that Anthony's doing, too? Was it his way of getting back at the center for taking a call from his niece? Or was there more to it than that?

What if he had been at the center looking for the phone records? What if he was trying to find out who it was that took the call? But Kennedy hadn't filled out any paperwork while she was there. Even if Jodie's uncle or one of his stooges broke into the center, how could he have known Kennedy was the one with the hotline cell? Then she remembered — Carl writing her name down on the big wall calendar, Kennedy jotting down her dorm room number on the purple Post-it. From there, it would have been easy enough for Anthony to find her room, check up on her

181

contacts, bug her phone. But would he really have gone through so much trouble to keep the press from learning about Jodie's pregnancy? Politicians' daughters got pregnant every day, didn't they? Of course, this would be more sensational since Jodie was so young and her father was the most conservative gubernatorial candidate the state may have ever seen, but it would pass, right? Nobody paid attention to the tabloids for that long. If the election wasn't in a week, would Kennedy still be sitting here today?

She thought about the internet search she had been doing when Dustin barged into her room. She was seconds away from calling Carl about her suspicions. How could Anthony have known? How could Dustin and Vinny have gotten there so fast? Unless they had been watching more than her phone. Kennedy's whole spine went rigid at the thought. So was all this to cover up the pregnancy, then? Or was there more to it? Incest? Statutory rape? Child abuse? She remembered Nick saying the press was lurking around St. Margaret's looking for a scandal. They would have gotten one, too, if Anthony's men hadn't caught Kennedy when they did.

Her thoughts about St. Margaret's led to others. If they bothered kidnapping Kennedy, why would they stop there? What if they went after Carl or Sandy, too? The Lindgrens had all the same information Kennedy did when she went to meet with Nick in his office.

Nick. She tried to think through their conversation. Had either of them mentioned the Abernathys? Wasn't it Nick who told her they went to St. Margaret's in the first place? If Anthony's men suspected Nick might reach the same conclusions as Kennedy, would they get rid of him, too?

Jodie shifted on the couch, and Kennedy rubbed her on the shoulder. "Are you holding up ok?" she asked. It was a stupid question. Nothing was ok about any of this.

"My feet are really cold."

Kennedy had just decided to risk Vinny's wrath by asking him for a blanket when his phone sounded again. This time he grunted and answered it reluctantly. "Hey, Anthony."

"That might be my uncle," Jodie whispered. Was that hope in her voice? "Do you think he's going to tell them to let us go?"

Was she still so naïve? Kennedy didn't want to lie. "I don't know." Kennedy couldn't believe Anthony tried to deceive Jodie into thinking those pills were anxiety meds. She tried to listen in to Vinny's conversation, but all she could catch were snippets of mumbled words that made no sense when strung together.

The door to the top of the stairs swung open. As Dustin

came down, Kennedy tried to guess how long he had been gone. Forty minutes? Maybe a little more. What did that tell her about their location? What did that mean about their chances of rescue or escape?

The starchy smell of French fries reached the bottom of the stairs before he did. He carried two McDonald's bags. Kennedy swallowed a whole mouthful of saliva as the fatty aroma swirled around in her empty stomach. When was the last time she had eaten? And how could she watch Dustin and Vinny dining in front of her when she was so hungry she hardly trusted her legs to support her weight anymore?

To her surprise, Dustin threw one of the McDonald's sacks at her when he passed by, along with a plastic shopping bag. Even if she wanted to, she couldn't ignore the greasy smell wafting up to her nostrils, so enticing she could almost taste it. She passed Jodie the package of pads when Vinny called out, "This time she goes by herself."

Kennedy didn't argue. "Think you can make it?" she asked.

Jodie nodded.

"Let me know if you need anything," she whispered when Vinny wasn't looking. "I'll save some of the food for you."

Jodie was walking more smoothly now. Kennedy's

fingers trembled as she broke the burger in half. It took all the self-control that she possessed to refrain from eating the entire meal. She finished her portion in a few ravenous bites and tucked the rest of the food away to save it for Jodie. Her hands still shook when she was done, but she reminded herself that Jodie would need the iron and the calories more than she did.

Vinny and Dustin were still eating their meals over by the table. What were they working on over there, anyway? Kennedy took advantage of the silence and tried to pray. She thanked God for providing the much-needed food and for helping Jodie feel a little better. After that, her mind was racing too fast to formulate any sort of cohesive request. She hoped God understood anyway. Didn't her dad say God knows what we need before we ask him?

There was a buzzing sound from upstairs, and Vinny turned to Dustin. "That's Anthony. Keep an eye on them." Vinny stomped up the stairs. So was Anthony actually here? Would he dare to show himself to his niece, or would he keep hiding behind his stooges like the coward he was?

Kennedy watched Dustin as he finished up the last of his fries. He must have sensed her staring, because he turned to her and announced with a full mouth, "She's still going to have to take those pills."

Kennedy wondered if Jodie could hear from the bathroom. How long was she going to take in there? Was she all right? "She can't do that. It's not safe." She tried to talk loud enough so Dustin could hear without having her words carry to every square inch of the room. Why couldn't he come closer?

Dustin shrugged. "Vinny's going now to talk to her uncle. She's taking them."

For a minute Kennedy wondered what would happen if she grabbed the pills and swallowed them herself. It couldn't be more dangerous for her than for Jodie, could it? But they would stop her before she could carry through. If she could only reason with them ...

Kennedy stood up, studying Dustin's expression as she took a few steps toward him. He kept eating, so she went a little farther until she was a foot or two away from the workbench. At least now she didn't have to yell across the room. She lowered her voice and kept her ear strained to hear when Jodie or Vinny returned. "Those pills only work when a girl is a few weeks pregnant. If you take them later than that ..." What would happen? Kennedy didn't know, so she'd have to bluff. "If you take them later than that, it's really dangerous for both the mom and the baby." That made sense, didn't it?

Dustin shrugged. Of course, he wouldn't care about the baby's life. But didn't he worry about what Anthony Abernathy would do if Jodie died or ended up in the hospital?

"If you don't believe me, I can look it up for you. Do you have internet down here?"

Dustin's eyes narrowed suspiciously.

"I'm telling you, those pills could kill her."

Dustin put down his fries. "You give me the information, and I'll look it up." There was a laptop computer on the far side of the work table, and Dustin drummed his fingers on the wooden platform while he waited for it to start.

"She said she's already five months along." Kennedy tried to keep her voice sounding reasonable, but now that she could see what was going on at the work bench, she grew even more nervous. Weapons were strewn across the wooden platform. Parts of guns, boxes of ammo. She tried not to stare as one incessant question raced through her mind — if Dustin planned to let her live, would he have allowed her to see his stockpile?

Kennedy glanced at the screen as it lit up and saw what looked like blueprints for a building. Was that where they were keeping her? If she got a chance to study it, could it teach her how to escape? Dustin quickly closed the browser and opened up a Yahoo search page. "Well?"

Kennedy couldn't remember the name of the drug. "Look up *abortion pills and second trimester*," she told him and shot a glance at the staircase. She was sure if Vinny came down now he would be furious to see her by the workbench. Dustin was staring at the keyboard while he typed, and if Kennedy had any idea what to do with a gun, she might have been able to grab one before he had time to react. What was the point of her and her dad watching all those action movies if she never learned the first thing about handling real weapons?

"All right." Dustin strained his neck forward as he stared at the screen.

Kennedy noticed he had misspelled most of the words in his search, but Yahoo still brought up the name of the pill she was looking for. "That one." She pointed. He squinted, and Kennedy saw a small knife on the table, gleaming in the bluish glow from the screen. Did she dare?

Dustin clicked on the link and then looked at Kennedy. "Now what?"

She got a little closer. Her fingers were near enough to brush the knife's leather sheath. "Click there, under *frequently asked questions*."

He stared blankly until she tapped the screen to show him

the FAQ tab.

She let her eyes skim the bullet points briefly. "There it is. See? The pills are only designed for use in the first seven weeks. She's way beyond that."

"How do you know?" he scowled.

"Well ... she told me."

Dustin let out a short laugh, but he shut up in an instant as soon as Vinny shouted down the staircase. Kennedy froze and wondered if he would be angrier at her for leaving the couch or at Dustin for letting her up in the first place. Would they cuff her again?

Dustin's eyes grew wide, and he scurried to the bottom of the steps. "What do you need?" He seemed as eager as she was to keep Vinny from coming downstairs.

Kennedy ignored the danger warnings screeching from her brain and grabbed the knife. She slipped it into her pocket seconds before Dustin came back to the bench.

"You need to get back to the couch," he told her in a low growl. She hurried as fast as she dared, wondering if the knife's outline would stick out and give her away. Should she hide it in between the cushions maybe? Why did they have to make jeans so tight these days? She tried to pull her sweater down to cover it.

She sank back on the couch as Jodie opened the

bathroom door and shuffled back to her seat. Kennedy hoped Jodie would be a little more comfortable now that she was cleaner. "Everything go all right?" she asked.

Jodie nodded and rubbed her arms. "Yeah. I'm just cold. And tired."

"Get some rest." Kennedy wondered how long they had before Vinny made her take those pills. After that, who knew what would happen? "You can lie down here again if you want."

Jodie put her head on Kennedy's lap. Kennedy bit her lip. *God, if you're listening at all, we're still here. And we're still waiting for that miracle.*

CHAPTER 19

Jodie was asleep by the time Vinny came back downstairs. He stomped louder than normal on the steps, and he cursed more vehemently than usual when he stepped on some sort of wrench that had fallen on the ground by the workbench. She couldn't hear what he and Dustin were fighting about in their hushed whispers, but she saw by their body language they were both angry. Not a good time to make either one of them more upset.

"Fine." Vinny spat and trudged to the couch, his large hands balled into fists that looked as hard as granite. Did he know about the knife? Had Dustin told him she had seen their weapon stash?

"Why'd you tell Dustin the pills won't work?"

They still thought she had some sort of medical expertise, so she did her best to pack confidence into her tone. "She's already in her second trimester. Those pills won't be effective at this stage." That would probably be a better deterrent than anything else. Kennedy watched him frown and quickly added, "It would be very dangerous for her, as well, since they're not designed for this late in the pregnancy."

"Her uncle told her to take them."

"I talked to her just a little bit ago." Kennedy kept her voice even. "She said she lied to her uncle about how far into the pregnancy she really was."

Vinny glared at the girl sleeping with her head on Kennedy's lap. What was he going to do to her? A protective instinct, stronger than hunger or fear or cold, surged from Kennedy's whole body. She pictured it wrapping itself all around Jodie while she slumbered, shielding her, comforting her. For a moment, Kennedy wondered if that's how her own mother felt toward her. Could you really live your whole life with such a strong desire to defend someone whose future and fate rested entirely out of your control? Wouldn't you go mad? *Please, God. Aren't you listening? Can't you do something?*

Vinny scowled. Kennedy's heart pounded in her chest, so loud she wondered if he could hear it. But a calming presence floated past her, a whisper of comfort breathed over her. Was this what Christians sometimes talked about when they said they felt the Holy Spirit?

There was no majestic opening of the heavens. There was no loud rumble of thunder. Her body still shivered until her back and abs were sore. But she felt invisible arms of protection covering her, spreading all the way over to Jodie, whose eyelids were almost translucent while she rested. Was God really here? Kennedy wondered if this was how the Secret Seminary students felt when they faced arrests or interrogation. Was this why they never showed fear? If the feeling could have converted itself into something tangible, she would have reached out to pocket it, saving it for whenever she needed it in the future.

She held her breath, certain something must happen soon. Maybe God would send an earthquake to crack open the walls and let Jodie and her escape. Hadn't he done something like that once in the Bible? Kennedy couldn't remember the details. Or maybe Vinny would have a heart attack and they could rush right by him and flag down someone to help. Or their rescuers could storm the place. Someone as well known as Jodie Abernathy couldn't go missing for long before every member of the police force was out looking, right?

Kennedy waited. Nothing. Vinny reached into his pocket. She knew what he was going to do before he pulled out the four white pills. The gentle awakening in her spirit passed, leaving her colder than before. She strained her senses. Could she catch the feeling once more before it deserted her forever?

Vinny cleared his throat. "Wake her up."

A harsh, biting winter replaced the peace from seconds ago. Kennedy doubted that any amount of prayer could ever warm her again. The air itself felt less dense, the room darker. The chill in her body seeped farther down into her bones.

"Wake her up," Vinny repeated.

Kennedy thought about the knife. Its image zipped through her mind before she could stop herself. Did she have the courage? Could she fight him off?

No. The thought didn't come from her. For a second, there was something almost familiar about it. The calming presence returned long enough to assure Kennedy she hadn't imagined the whole thing. It deserted her as fast and unexpectedly as it came, but there wasn't room for doubt. *No.*

Something was tugging at her heart — an invitation to trust. A chance to let go of her own ideas, her own self-reliance. A picture flashed in her mind of a giant canyon. There was no bridge offering easy passage across, but there was a path going through it. Through the thorns that

194

threatened to scratch and cut into her skin. Through the darkness that clung to her like a winter chill. Through the heaviness of mourning, the weightiness of grief. There was no bridge, but there was a path, dangerous, rocky, terrifying.

Kennedy shook Jodie. "You need to wake up now."

CHAPTER 20

Jodie's eyes blinked open. "What?" She sounded groggy, like Kennedy's roommate Willow did nearly every weekend when she finally woke up.

"They want you to take the pills now." Kennedy tried to seize some of the peace, some of the comfort from before and wrap her words up in it. She didn't know how or why, but she knew — as certainly as she knew that the earth was round or that her parents loved her — things would work out all right. Was there a way to make Jodie believe it, too?

Lord, please give her that same comfort. Give her the same trust. Unfortunately, it was yet another prayer whispered in vain.

Jodie clutched Kennedy's arm. "I don't want those."

Kennedy stroked her hair. "I know." What else was there to say? "I know."

"I can't."

Vinny let out a huff of air. "Enough whining. Now do it."

"I can't," Jodie repeated, shaking her head weakly from side to side.

"I told you ..." Vinny roared, but he didn't get to finish. A high-pitched squeal sounded, louder than any smoke detector Kennedy had ever heard. Both she and Jodie clasped their hands to their ears. A red light on the wall strobed, making shadows dance and flicker. Vinny muttered angrily under his breath and raced to the workbench. Dustin had already grabbed one of the guns and was sprinting up the steps. Vinny snatched two others and rushed right behind him.

Kennedy freed her arm from Jodie's clutches. If she didn't act now, she would never have the courage. She sucked in her breath, leapt up from the couch, and dashed to the laptop. *Please start up. Please start up.*

The screen lit within seconds. Kennedy let out the air she had been holding. She forgot all about the pills. She forgot all about the serenity God had poured out over her spirit a few minutes earlier. She had only one mission.

A browser was open to some sort of list. If there was more time, she might have tried to figure out what it was. She opened a new tab and typed in the web address for St. Margaret's, mentally chiding Carl for not giving his church a shorter name. What would Vinny do to her if he came downstairs now? It didn't matter. She had to find a way to get Jodie free. The siren blared. The screeching noise fired agony into her ears. She had to move fast. As soon as the webpage came up, she clicked on tab to leave a comment. She didn't know if the messages went right to Carl or to some receptionist, but that didn't matter as long as it got to someone fast. She had to tell them where she was. As far as Carl knew, she was really busy with school, and her voice was too hoarse to allow her to talk on the phone. Her fingers trembled as they flew over the keyboard. It took all of her self-control to leave the misspellings there instead of wasting the time to correct them.

It's Kennedy. I'm here with Jodie A. Two men are keeping us in a basement.

There was so much more to say. She wanted to tell him how long of a drive it took to get there. She wanted to tell him that when Dustin went to the store, it was a little over half an hour before he returned. She wanted to tell him the names and descriptions of the men involved, including Anthony Abernathy. But there was no time. If either of the men came down and saw her at the laptop …

She clicked the send button only to have the computer protest because she hadn't entered a valid email. She grumbled at the website designer, then blasted in her address

— typos and all — and exited out of the browser. For a second, she worried that she had also closed down the page Dustin and Vinny had up, but there it was again. Some sort of itinerary, maybe? She wondered if she should switch the laptop to sleep mode or if it was better to let the screensaver start on its own. Why hadn't she thought of that before? If they saw the screen on now, they would know she had done something. For a moment, she considered cuffing herself back by the couch so if they accused her, she could deny it. But of course they would remember if she were handcuffed when they left. Wouldn't they?

Her heart was throbbing when she got back to the couch, and her stomach was twisted in a knot. For the first time, she was glad she hadn't eaten that other half of the burger. Her legs were weak and unsteady, like stalks of limp celery.

Jodie stared at her wide-eyed, her hands still over her ears. "What's going on?"

Kennedy wished she knew. The alarm continued to shriek. Had someone broken into the complex? Was that why the men both grabbed their guns before they raced upstairs? Or could this be some sort of a drill? If it was an attack, did the men plan to leave the two girls down here to fend for themselves? Kennedy wished the siren would stop, but she didn't want Dustin or Vinny to come downstairs until the laptop's screensaver kicked in again. And what would she say if they noticed something was different about the computer? What if they questioned her? Was there any sort of excuse she could come up with to stay out of trouble? Her lungs constricted, and she had to force air in and out of her chest while her mind raced through its different options. What if she told them she was worried about Jodie and went online to research medical conditions that might cause her bleeding? She glanced over. Jodie's skin tone had improved. Her eyes looked tired and nervous, but she didn't appear to be experiencing any pain or discomfort.

Could she tell them she had an assignment due today and was checking up on the status of one of her classes? No one would believe that a hostage, however much of a perfectionist, would sneak onto a laptop to check on homework. The only thing to do was hope that either the screensaver would kick in on time or they would be so worked up over the alarm they wouldn't notice.

"Why did they run upstairs?" Jodie asked.

"I don't know." For a minute, she considered telling Jodie this was all some sort of a drill. But what if it really was a rescue attempt? What if someone had noticed one of them missing and tracked them to the complex? Someone could have followed Anthony Abernathy if he came here earlier to talk to Vinny. Someone may have witnessed Kennedy's abduction on the side of the road. And of course, if anyone realized that Senator Abernathy's daughter was kidnapped, the city would throw all its resources into finding her as soon as possible.

Now that sirens were shrieking in her ears and the red strobe light was pulsing pain to the back of her head, Kennedy almost wished things were back how they had been. She didn't know what was going to happen. She didn't know if whatever battle might be raging upstairs would work its way to the basement or not. She thought about the weapons stockpiled on the workbench. How long could Vinny and Dustin hold off a rescue team?

She stood up. "I wonder if we should go wait in the bathroom." She tried to think of something to say to keep Jodie from feeling frightened. No matter how fast her heart was racing, no matter how her lungs burst at the thought of fresh air, this might be some sort of a drill or internal conflict. Still, she wanted to get Jodie someplace a little safer, a little more protected. "Maybe we could find a way to clean up your clothes."

Jodie didn't answer. Her eyes were wide, and her hand was cold when Kennedy helped her to her feet. "Do you hurt at all?" They shuffled toward the bathroom, and she wished

Jodie would hurry. Kennedy's whole body was tense, and her ears strained over the alarm for the gunshots she expected to explode behind her at any minute.

When they got to the bathroom, Kennedy shut the door behind them. There wasn't anything she could use as a barricade. Now what? Jodie looked up at her with trusting eyes, and Kennedy's heart felt like it had been wrung dry. *Lord, how am I supposed to help her? How am I supposed to help either of us?* She remembered the peace that covered her before the alarm sounded. Why couldn't she carry that calm around with her all the time? She wondered if other Christians, more mature believers, lived their entire lives in a constant state of awe, perpetually aware of the presence of the Holy Spirit. She thought about people like the Lindgrens or the Secret Seminary students. What would they do if they were here now? Sing hymns? Drop to their knees in prayer? The only thing Kennedy felt capable of doing was throwing up.

"Oh." The color drained from Jodie's face.

"Are you all right?"

"I think I need to pee."

Kennedy faced the door to give Jodie some privacy. She almost offered to step out and wait, but her hands grew clammy at the thought of going back into the room where that red light sent shadows dancing wildly across the walls. The grease from the fast food she had eaten threatened to turn against her. "Take as long as you need," she told Jodie. "I don't mind."

What was going on upstairs? When would Dustin and Vinny come down? What would they say when they found both girls in the bathroom? Kennedy hoped the screensaver had kicked in by now. At any rate, she would rather have them mad at her for taking Jodie to the toilet than for tampering with their computer.

Jodie made a little moaning noise.

"Is everything all right?" Kennedy asked without turning around.

The tiny little *yes* that answered back was anything but convincing.

Dear God, Kennedy prayed. She was sick of asking for rescue. She was sick of experiencing tiny glimpses of peace that didn't last. She was sick of trying to maintain a trusting, positive attitude when the whole world around her was spiraling down to hell and madness.

Dear God, she began again, *just get us out of here.*

CHAPTER 21

"Maybe it was a fluke."

Kennedy's spine stiffened when she heard Dustin's voice. There was a series of six short beeps, but Kennedy's ears still rang even after the alarm fell silent.

"You don't get flukes with a ten-grand security system," Vinny grumbled.

"It might have been nothing." Kennedy detected a sort of questioning hopefulness in Dustin's tone. "Hey, where'd they go?"

Kennedy's spine tingled as footsteps neared the bathroom, and she jumped a little when someone pounded on the door.

"We're almost done," Kennedy called out quickly, afraid they might barge in.

"Get outta there." Vinny pounded on the door again. "Now."

Somehow, he was less intimidating when she didn't have

to look at his face. "She's not feeling well." Kennedy opened the door a crack and slipped out so he wouldn't feel compelled to come in.

"What's wrong with her now?"

"She's been on the toilet since the alarm went off." Kennedy could judge by Vinny's expression that she shouldn't have mentioned the sirens. "I think she's passing a lot of blood," she hastened to add.

Vinny shrugged. "That's why Dustin went to the store. Give her a pad and get back to the couch."

Kennedy gripped the doorknob, clenching her teeth to keep her mouth shut.

"And be quick about it." Vinny's warning made her blood seethe, but she turned around, swallowing her contempt.

Jodie hadn't moved but sat on the toilet with her eyes closed.

"They need you to get dressed again." She hated to rush Jodie, but she didn't want to get Vinny more upset. He was tense enough already, like a shaken can of soda about to burst under all that extra pressure. She looked around the room. "Do you need another pad?"

Jodie grimaced, as if the sound of Kennedy's voice hurt her ears. She held her finger up for silence. Kennedy waited.

Was she getting worse?

Kennedy walked over to the toilet and put her hand on Jodie's shoulder. Jodie sucked in her breath at the touch.

"What's wrong?" Kennedy had a hard time keeping the panic out of her voice. She looked down. The water in the toilet bowl was dark red. For the second time in the past ten minutes, Kennedy regretted eating such a greasy meal.

Jodie whimpered when Kennedy tried to help her to her feet.

Kennedy let go. "Vinny says you need to come out." How could she get Jodie up?

"I can't," Jodie squeaked.

Kennedy felt dizzy. *This is just like school,* she told herself. *It's like studying for a math test when you have over a hundred pages of reading, a paper, and a lab all due the next day.* Panic was a luxury she simply couldn't afford. She had to assess the problem, figure out what needed to be done, and take care of everything so her world kept on spinning. That's all this was. Just like school. The setting was different, the teachers more cruel, and the stakes were measured in human lives instead of grade point averages, but the route to success was exactly the same.

"Can you tell me what's wrong? Where do you hurt?"

Jodie put her hand on her stomach. Kennedy did the

same and felt it tighten up like a concrete ball drying in fast-motion. Jodie grimaced and shut her eyes again.

"It's going to be all right." Kennedy forced herself to smile even though Jodie wasn't looking at her and wouldn't have noticed. "I'm going to get you a new pad, and then I'm going to help you get back to the couch."

"Get out," Vinny declared, and Kennedy only had enough time to position herself between the toilet and the door before he barged in.

"She's not ready!" Kennedy spread out her arms, as if that would give Jodie an extra measure of privacy.

"I said time's up," Vinny snarled.

Kennedy didn't want to move. She wanted to stay there as at least a partial shield blocking Vinny's view, but she couldn't help Jodie from where she was. *Please, God. Can't you just make him go away?*

Kennedy had lost count of how many prayers God had failed to answer so far today. Blinking back tears of angry frustration, she walked toward the wall and pulled out a new pad from the package in the corner. Jodie's eyes were still closed, and Kennedy wondered if she realized Vinny was in there with them at all.

"Come on," Kennedy urged. "We need to get you up."

Jodie was taking short, shallow breaths. Tiny pearls of

sweat beaded on her brow.

"What's her problem?" Vinny demanded, and Kennedy imagined how rewarding it would be to watch him get shot point-blank like in the movies. She was surprised by the heat of her hatred. Had she grown so vengeful she could actually wish him dead?

Yes, she could.

"I think she might be ..." Kennedy lowered her voice to keep Jodie from overhearing, even though she doubted Jodie was paying attention to anything. "I think she might be miscarrying."

Vinny shrugged. "Good."

Didn't he understand? Didn't he realize? There was no way Kennedy could deal with a medical crisis of this magnitude. Anger boiled up in her gut like the contents of a pressure cooker. "No, that's not good. This little girl is five months pregnant, and she's hemorrhaging in this filthy bathroom."

"She's not hemorrhaging," Vinny remarked, and Kennedy wondered if he knew the meaning of the word.

As if on cue, Jodie let out a little groan, and Kennedy heard something plop into the toilet.

Vinny snapped his head back to Kennedy, his nose wrinkled up, his eyes darting from her to the bowl. "What was that?"

"I think it might have been a blood clot." She braced her queasy stomach and peeked down to confirm her suspicions.

Jodie was ashen. She gripped her midsection. Kennedy reached out to tell her to try to relax when Jodie shifted her position slightly.

"You need to get her to a hospital. Now." Kennedy stood as tall as she could, even though her leg muscles quivered and threatened to buckle right out from under her.

"But the baby's dead, you say?"

Couldn't he see Jodie was in trouble? Did he have no conscience, no sense of remorse or compassion? Kennedy had heard stories from the North Korean refugees in Yanji about horrifically evil people, but somehow in her mind she had compartmentalized those villains. They lived in dictatorships. They thrived in nations with godless, immoral laws and horrific records of human-rights abuses. Not in America. Not in big cities like Cambridge or Boston. And they didn't prey on girls like Kennedy and Rose, girls from Harvard, girls from important families, girls from churched backgrounds.

She reached out and felt Jodie's forehead. It was cool and clammy. Even her skin had a strange, sick-smelling odor that immediately reminded Kennedy of those horrible visits so long ago with her grandmother in the hospital. She brought her hand back and balled it into a fist, hoping Vinny couldn't see how much she trembled.

"She's losing way too much blood. She has to get medical treatment."

"But the baby's taken care of?" Vinny pressed. Was that all these monsters cared about? A dead fetus so Wayne Abernathy could continue his political career? Was murdering a child a reasonable price to pay to avoid a scandal? And even if Vinny had no regard for the baby's life, didn't he care that Jodie could bleed to death in his disgusting, germ-infested bathroom?

"I don't know." Kennedy felt like throwing up her hands but kept them planted firmly at her sides. "I'm not a doctor." Couldn't he see how serious this was? The pointed sheath in her pocket jabbed into her leg. She envisioned herself wielding the knife, demanding that Vinny take Jodie to a hospital, but her mind answered back with a snapshot of their arsenal of weapons in various stages of assembly on the workbench. A move like that would be suicide. And if something happened to Kennedy, Jodie would lose the only advocate she had left.

"I don't feel good." Jodie reached her arm out and used Kennedy's shoulder to hoist herself up a little. Kennedy tried to adjust her position to block the child from Vinny's view. If he wasn't going to help, couldn't he grant them some privacy? Kennedy tried to think back to her physiology unit in AP Biology from high school. What were you supposed to do if someone was losing that much blood? She couldn't think of any answer except get them to the emergency room as fast as possible.

Jodie raised herself up but stayed positioned over the toilet. There was too much blood. Too many clots. Even if she had been wearing pads, Kennedy guessed she would have soaked through several just in the past few minutes. For the first time, she was glad Vinny was still here. Couldn't he see?

He wrinkled his nose. "You two will have to clean up the mess when this is over." He turned to leave.

"I can't ..." Jodie's face was the shade of chalk dust. Her eyelids fluttered. Her pupils rolled up until for a second only the whites showed. Her body swayed. The scene played before Kennedy like freeze-frame animation, displaying itself in millisecond shots one after another. Jodie reached toward Kennedy before she swung off balance. Kennedy's muscles weren't ready to support her extra weight. They both dropped to the floor, and Kennedy's knee took the brunt of both their falls.

"Are you all right? Sweetie, what's wrong?"

Jodie's head lay in her lap again, but it wasn't anything like a little bit ago when they rested together on the couch. This time, Jodie's eyes weren't closed in the heavy slumber of the weary. She had passed out, the gravity of her condition written in the pallor of her sickly gray face. Kennedy stared at Jodie's chest and counted five awful, spirit-draining seconds before it rose. She held the girl's clammy wrist. Her weak, fluttering pulse reminded Kennedy of a dying butterfly's last desperate attempt at flight.

In the silence that followed, Kennedy could hear Vinny swallow. "I'll go call her uncle."

CHAPTER 22

The next few minutes could have lasted an hour or more. When Vinny left the room, the unmistakable feeling of total isolation weighed down Kennedy's whole body. What if Jodie died? How much blood could a person lose and still survive? She sucked in her breath at the sight of the puddle pooling around Jodie's body and knew they were in need of a miracle.

She lay Jodie's head flat on the ground, hoping to keep some of the blood going to her brain. Wasn't there something about elevating the legs as well? Or would that cause more blood to flow out? She wasn't sure. Her fingers never left Jodie's wrist, and she fully expected that frantic flutter to cease any minute. How long could your heart keep up such an impossible pace? She knew the basics of CPR but had never taken a class. And was it different on an adult than it would be for a child?

A child. A child who should have never been pregnant in

the first place. A child who should have never found herself a pawn in this dangerous political game, where her family members held no regard for her safety. What had her uncle been thinking? Even if it wasn't the pills he prescribed that did this to Jodie, Kennedy would hold him guilty for it. All of it. No thirteen-year-old should be forced to endure a fraction of the trauma Jodie had suffered.

Kennedy thought about the articles from her dad's pro-life magazines. She thought about all those testimonies, victims of rape who carried their babies to term and found room in their hearts to love and nurture them. Or the story Willow told her about the lady who died because she delayed cancer treatment that would have killed her child. Kennedy felt like the biggest hypocrite who had ever volunteered to work for a pregnancy center. She couldn't find room in her heart to worry about the baby. She only had the energy and psychological fortitude to care about one thing right now, and one thing only — Jodie's safety. If she ever saw Carl or Sandy again, the first thing she would do was resign her position at the center, insignificant as it was.

The seconds passed. The puddle of blood widened, seeping into Jodie's shirt, creeping its way toward Kennedy's shoes while she crouched on the floor. In eight years, Kennedy would have the medical skills necessary to handle situations far worse than this. She would know exactly what to do. She could save Jodie's life. Maybe even the baby's. But time wouldn't hold still until she got her medical degree. This emergency was happening right now. Kennedy was just a first-year in college. An undergrad. She had never set foot in a med-school class. She had never completed a single rotation. She had no idea how to start an IV, how to stop a patient from hemorrhaging. She didn't know how many chest compressions you were supposed to do during CPR. And she still didn't really understand what she was doing here. Had God allowed her to be kidnapped just so she could care for Jodie? Why couldn't he have kept them both safe in the first place?

Her body trembled violently, as if all those prayers the Lord left unanswered that day sat festering in her blood like a toxin. Her teeth chattered noisily, her breathing grew shallower. What would Vinny say if he came back to find Jodie and her both passed out on the floor? And what in the world was she supposed to do now? Even if she knew a way to help Jodie, even if she possessed the magic knowledge it would take to stop her bleeding or save the baby inside her, how could she execute any of those lofty plans when it felt like she was going to suffocate?

Kennedy gasped noisily in time with her shivers. The blood beneath Jodie widened with each passing minute. Kennedy had to fight the irrational fear that she would faint dead away if the puddle made it all the way to where she squatted. How many blood-borne pathogens were there, and what were the chances of someone as young as Jodie carrying one of them? Careful not to let her sleeves drip down, she swept her hand against Jodie's forehead and had to watch her chest for the next ten breaths to assure herself the girl was still alive. She was so cold to the touch, it was almost as if Kennedy had reached out and encountered death's forerunner seated on Jodie's brow.

"She's in here."

Kennedy never expected Vinny's voice to bring such a surge of relief. She tried to stand up but was too dizzy. How had she gotten so weak? Was it actually her blood pooling all around them, her life source draining out of her in a steady, unstoppable stream?

"What'd you do to her?"

Kennedy had never seen Jodie's uncle before, but he had the same build, the same hairline, the same square jaw as his brother. He was taller than Vinny and skinnier, someone who might have passed for a male model if he were ten or fifteen years younger, or the kind of actor who would make

216

middle-aged housewives swoon.

"What happened?"

Kennedy didn't know if Anthony was talking to her or not. Either way, she didn't have the strength to respond.

"We think she's having a miscarriage." Vinny's voice lost a little bit of its brusque edge as he glanced up at Anthony Abernathy.

"So you got her to take the pills after all?" It was worded like a question but came out definitively like a statement.

"No, this happened before the pills."

Kennedy wondered if Vinny was going to tell him about the fight, about how he fell on top of Jodie. She doubted it.

Anthony shrugged. "Well, it got taken care of one way or another." He spoke casually, as if someone had made plans to take the subway but ended up hopping on a bus instead. "Now why's she on the floor like that?"

"She's hemorrhaging." Kennedy's voice came out steadier than she expected. "She needs to see a doctor."

Jodie's uncle frowned. "Unfortunately, I don't think that's possible. What can you do for her from here?"

I've already done everything I can think of, Kennedy wanted to scream. Which was basically nothing except for lowering Jodie's head so the blood didn't have to travel against gravity to get to her brain.

"She passed out from all the blood loss. She's ..."

"Yes, I hear that's natural with miscarriages." Was he even listening? Did he care? Or would he stand here and watch his niece bleed to death? "I'll send Dustin out for some ibuprofen. That might help if she wakes up with cramps."

"She's not sleeping!" This time Kennedy did allow her voice to rise. "She passed out. She may already be in shock." A blanket. Why hadn't Kennedy thought to cover her up with a blanket? It's what the first responders always did in the suspense novels she read, at least.

Anthony frowned. If he gave her another shrug, it might invigorate her enough that she could summon all her strength and attack him with her bare hands.

"Look at the toilet." Kennedy pointed. "Look how much blood she's lost in there. That's on top of all this." She gestured to the floor. "And that's just from the past ten minutes or so."

Jodie's uncle fingered his chin. "That's a lot." He said it thoughtfully, as if they were discussing a late commuter rail. "But a fetus that small should pass easily enough." He scratched his chin again.

He still had no idea.

"Her baby is five months old. She's over halfway through the pregnancy." Kennedy's voice was steady, but she felt like she was screaming at a small child who refused to accept common-sense reason.

At this point, Kennedy expected one of two things to occur. Anthony would either maintain his stoic demeanor and refuse his niece medical care, or he would spring into action and make rapid plans to get her the attention she needed.

He did neither.

His indifferent stare morphed almost instantaneously. The dull, apathetic eyes narrowed, boring hatred into his niece's body. The muscles in his face and neck all seemed to flex at once, making some of the veins pop up underneath the smooth skin. The formerly calm, placid voice was now laced with disgust. "The lying little brat."

His alteration occurred so dramatically, his words spewed out so vehemently that Kennedy nearly lost her balance. Still managing to maintain her squat, she stuck out both arms so she wouldn't topple onto the dirty floor. She had no idea what brought about the sudden change, but she understood now why Jodie lied to him about the pregnancy.

Anthony stomped out of the bathroom, nearly plowing Vinny over on his way. He stormed back a few paces later. "Five months you said?"

Kennedy bit her lip. She wanted to believe Jodie was

telling the truth about her relationship with Samir. Now she wasn't so sure. Maybe the two kids really had been together. Had she just betrayed Jodie's trust? Well, the uncle had to know at this point. He had to realize how serious this was.

Anthony kept pacing and lifted his eyes to the ceiling. A few seconds later, he punched the wall, exclaiming more loudly, "Five months!"

A tiny gurgle of a cough made them all fall silent and lean toward Jodie.

"Is she waking up?" Vinny asked.

They stared expectantly for several seconds, but there was no more movement. Kennedy kept her eyes on the girl's chest, as if she could keep Jodie's lungs functioning by sheer willpower.

"She needs a hospital," Kennedy whispered.

"She doesn't deserve it." Anthony resumed pacing the length of the bathroom in two strides at a time, swinging his arms as he went. Vinny had to avoid him more than once. "To think of all that planning, the lengths I went to cover up for a deceitful little ..."

So was he going to let her die, then? Is that how this was all going to end?

"Five months." Anthony shook his head and muttered under his breath. "So she was with him that whole time. The sneaky, conniving, spoiled brat. Five months."

Kennedy did her best to keep from getting in the way of his boots as he paced. For a minute, she imagined what would happen if he slipped in the puddle of blood. The whole scene played out like a bad *Three Stooges* sketch. Only there was no comedy in this drama.

"She lied to everyone." Anthony slowed down and crossed his arms. "If she had told me the truth ..." He glanced at Kennedy. For a moment, his eyes reflected a pained, tortured sadness. He shook his head, and the tenderness was replaced with calculating malice. "If she wasn't family, I'd let her bleed to death right here."

For the first time in her life, Kennedy realized how grateful she was for her own mom and dad, how glad she was that her definition of *family* bore no resemblance to Anthony Abernathy's.

He bumped into Vinny's shoulder when he started to pace again. "She's been with that toad this whole time. I told her parents that little Muslim was no good. They should have sent him to Vermont as soon as I told them to, then this wouldn't ..." He shook his head and waved his hand in the air dismissively. "Take her to the hospital. And tell her that if she even drops a hint as to who she really is, I will find her Arab boyfriend, and I will murder him. Got that?"

Vinny bent down, and Kennedy wanted to protest before he jostled Jodie up in his arms. Shouldn't they call the paramedics instead? Shouldn't they have a stretcher and someone trained to transport patients in such critical condition? But there was nothing she could say. At least Jodie would get the help she needed. Kennedy hoped it wouldn't be too late.

"Well, that's out of the way," Anthony growled, fixing his gaze on Kennedy. "Now get up. You're coming with me."

CHAPTER 23

Kennedy's mind processed the danger before her body had a chance to fully respond. She slapped Anthony's hand away when he reached out. He lunged and grabbed a handful of her hair. She barely managed to break his hold.

Scampering backward, she made it to the wall before he seized her collar and yanked her to her feet.

All those videos her dad made her watch on self-defense were a complete waste of time. How could she be prepared for something like this? How could she fight back when she only felt like throwing up or curling into a ball and trying to disappear into the air?

He tightened his hold, and her collar cut into her throat. She tried to swing herself around. He was too strong. She aimed a clumsy kick at his shin that did nothing to loosen his grip.

"You think fighting's going to get you anywhere?"

She choked back her scream and pictured Jodie's

unconscious body being carried out of their prison. She would get the medical attention she needed. At least she wasn't here to witness her uncle's brutality.

White spots floated in Kennedy's field of vision. She tried to reach back and claw at his face, but his hold was too tight. Would she pass out now, too?

She thought about the knife in her pocket. Did she dare use it? Could she ever find the intestinal fortitude? She glanced down at the blood clots on the floor. Bile rose in her throat.

"Let go of me." She scratched at his forearm and felt like a schnauzer fighting off a grizzly.

"You should have never gotten involved in any of this."

She tried to turn her face away from his nauseating breath.

"It was never your business to poke around in," he snarled.

Kennedy's head felt like it was about to float up like a helium balloon. She clutched at the front of her shirt, trying to give herself some breathing room. She could hardly think straight. The battle was lost. It had been lost the minute Anthony entered the room.

He turned his neck and bellowed out the door. "Dustin. Get over here. Now."

The younger man appeared seconds later. "Yeah?"

"Once we clean up here, you're going to Vermont. Take care of that Arab boy."

Dustin nodded. Kennedy was terrified to see him leave. She would have rather faced a hundred Dustins instead of one angry Anthony.

"Jodie said they were never really together." The words squeaked out of Kennedy's mouth.

She felt Anthony shrug behind her. "She lied."

Was Dustin going to go kill him, then? No, there was no way these men planned to let her live. She knew too much. She had seen too much. She thought of her parents, how devastated they would be. How long until they learned the truth? She wondered if Reuben or Willow would really grieve, or if it would only weird them out to have known the victim of a brutal murder. Her only consolation was that Jodie had made it out safely.

"Why?" Kennedy croaked. She had to get him talking more. She had to keep his mind on anything but her. She had to breathe. "Why are you doing any of this?"

Anthony's laugh fell flat in the room. "Jodie is my niece. I love her like she was my own flesh and blood."

There was something in his tone — something almost possessive — that made Kennedy shiver. Should she expect

ALANA TERRY

any less from a beast like this? It didn't matter. As long as he kept babbling, she could inhale. As long as he kept babbling, his attention and his wrath weren't focused solely on her.

"You know if this gets out, it's going to hurt her dad's campaign even more than the pregnancy would have."

He sniggered. "You think I'm doing this to help my brother?" His words dripped with cruelty. Did men like this really exist outside of horror novels? Did men like this have souls, or were they empty shells possessed by fiends and demons, intent on wreaking havoc on anyone and anything unfortunate enough to get in their way?

"Come on. Get moving." He nudged her forward without releasing his hold.

Kennedy glanced down and took a careful step around the bloody sea on the floor. What was going to happen now? It was like waking up from one nightmare only to fall back to sleep and dream something horrifically worse.

Anthony's voice held a hint of malicious humor. "You know, you shouldn't ask so many questions. One day you might learn something that …"

His boot skidded in the puddle of blood. His arms flailed out. One foot slipped out from under him. He crashed to the messy ground, knocking Kennedy over with him. Her reflexes were quicker than his, and she jumped out of his way before he could get up.

"Don't move." The force in her own voice startled her. The knife was out of her pocket, out of its sheath before she could change her mind. She held it out with a shaking hand and backed another step closer to the door.

He made a move to stand, but she tightened her grip on the weapon.

"I said don't move."

Anthony's eyes widened, and then he let out a laugh that rang out and echoed eerily against the walls. "Or what?"

Kennedy felt the blood drain from her face. Why had she brought a weapon into this deadly scenario? How many seconds would it take him to seize it and use it against her? Would she bleed more or less than Jodie when he was done?

Anthony narrowed his eyes angrily. "What are you going to do, girlie? Stab me to death?" Another laugh, like two pieces of silverware scraping against each other, setting her teeth on edge.

What should she do now? What could she do? She was about to risk an impossible dash out the bathroom when she heard the door by the stairs crash open.

"FBI!" A whole army of voices burst out at once. They shouted, made loud demands as a horde of boots stampeded down the stairs. How many were there? A dozen? A hundred?

"Drop your weapon!"

Two single pops sounded, and Kennedy let the knife clatter to the floor. Instinct told her to fall to the ground, but she wanted to stay as far away from Anthony as she could. She sucked in her breath and pressed against the wall.

Everything after that happened all at once. There was no slowing down the perception of time like she read about in books. First, Anthony swiped the knife and sprang to his feet. He spun around behind Kennedy and held the blade to her throat.

A second later, at least half a dozen men in dark gas masks materialized in the doorway, aiming assault rifles at them both.

CHAPTER 24

"Sir, drop the knife."

The rest of the team fell silent, and only the man in front spoke. His tone was calmer now, even though Kennedy's ears still rang with the sounds of the men's angry bellows and ultimatums from a moment earlier.

Anthony wrapped one arm around her chest. She could feel him breathing hard behind her and wasn't sure if she was the one quivering so much or both of them. She held her breath, trying to creep away from the blade pressed against her skin.

"Sir, you need to drop the knife. Now."

Kennedy wondered why the agent was so reserved. Couldn't he see what was happening? Couldn't he tell she was less than half an inch away from death? How far down was her carotid artery? And once Anthony made the fatal slice, how long would it take to die? Would it feel like drowning? Would it be peaceful, like falling to sleep as the world around you slowly went black? Or chaotic — gasping for nothing as you felt your life spurt out of you pulse by pulse?

The men in the doorway looked to Kennedy more like one cohesive unit of death than individual men. Their eyes were all fixed on Anthony. She wished one of them would look at her. They were trained for rescues like this, right? So why weren't they acting? Should she duck so they could get their shot? They must have good aim and quick reflexes. They'd make sure to hold their fire until she was out of the way.

Wouldn't they?

"Hold still." The leader was talking to her even though his eyes hadn't moved off of Anthony. Had he anticipated her thoughts? Why couldn't someone tell her what was going on? A little nod, a slight hand gesture — something to convince her they were going to take care of her?

Kennedy was trembling so hard she feared she might slice herself open on the blade. She could feel the cold pressure against her skin, but it hadn't cut into her yet. At least she didn't think it had. These men wouldn't let Anthony go that far, right?

Why were they so still?

"Don't take another step closer, or I'll kill her." Anthony

was still breathing heavily, but his voice didn't quiver.

"You'd be dead before you finished."

The words didn't comfort Kennedy at all. What did these men care more about — getting Anthony, or keeping her safe? When she stared into their hard, calculating faces, she had serious doubts. This wasn't anything like in the movies. There was no fast-paced soundtrack, no pops of gunfire syncopating in the background. In fact, it was almost completely silent except for the sound of her heartbeat pounding in her ears.

Anthony gripped her more tightly from behind. The movement from the men in black was barely perceptible. She didn't know if she actually saw it or only sensed the increase in tension. She sucked in her breath. Were they going to shoot? Was he going to cut? She knew too much. Even if Anthony was about to die, what would stop him from taking her down with him?

Apparently, the team leader's thoughts weren't that far from hers. "We have a medical team assembled right outside this building," he told Anthony. Kennedy knew she should feel relieved, but then again she didn't relish the thought of getting cut open at all. Was he trying to boost her confidence? "The girl would get immediate attention. And you would rot in hell. Your choice."

Anthony let out a loud sigh. Hope tried to emerge from its steel cocoon where Kennedy had buried it deep within.

"All right." Some of the tension seeped out of Anthony's strained muscles. "We'll do this your way."

Kennedy waited. Wasn't there supposed to be a rush of relief like they talked about in books? Shouldn't the men's faces relax? If she had to guess, their expressions were even more strained now. Or was it her imagination? Was the worst really over?

He removed his arm from across her chest.

"Easy," the team leader warned, but Kennedy didn't know which one of them he was talking to. What was she supposed to do now? Was she really free? "Easy ..."

She didn't trust her legs and waited for some sort of sign from her rescuers. If Anthony was letting her go, why did he still hold the blade to her neck?

"Lower that knife." The rescuer sounded like someone telling the high tide to calm itself and take a time out.

Hope for freedom merged with some sort of primitive, fear-laced instinct. Kennedy held her breath as Anthony slowly moved the knife away from her throat. So he really was giving in. It was over.

A second later, the saturated silence was broken by a chaotic din as everything erupted into noise at once.

Someone shouting, "No!" A dozen gunshots or more. The sound of Kennedy's own scream.

Next the shock of fiery, glowing, diabolical pain as Anthony plunged the knife into her back.

CHAPTER 25

There were voices, murmurs that sounded like they were coming from underwater. Tension. Worry. Would the nightmare never cease?

A high-pitched electronic wailing. Ceaseless. Relentless. Enough to drive you crazy if you let it.

Pain everywhere. Hot pain, as if a fiery lance still sizzled inside her. Over and over and over again.

People shouting commands. Hands poking here, prodding there. She wasn't ready to wake up yet.

"Kennedy? Sweetie? Can you hear me?"

The voice pulled her out of some dark, murky mire. She returned slowly, reluctantly. The light overhead burned. Why was someone shining the sun in her eyes?

"She's waking up." The gush of enthusiasm sounded out of place as the nightmare begrudgingly loosened its hold.

She blinked. Her eyes were even scratchier than normal.

"It's me, sweetie. Sandy. And Carl's here, too." The

voice was pleasant, kind. If Kennedy had any tears left in her ducts, she might have let them flow.

A hand held hers. A voice, strong as the wind. Bold as the ocean. "We're glad to have you back."

She tried to focus. Carl. She didn't recognize where she was. Was this the next chapter of the nightmare, a short reprieve before it dragged her back down in its clutches to the abyss?

"You're all right, sweetie." Sandy swept some hair off Kennedy's brow. "You're going to recover just fine."

"You're a very lucky young lady." Carl beamed at her with a sort of paternal pride.

"What time is it?" The words made sense in her mind, but she couldn't tell if they came out right.

"Excuse me." At the sound of the authoritative voice, Carl and Sandy stepped aside. A man in a police uniform strode over to Kennedy's bed. "I'm Detective Drisklay. I see you're waking up." He took a noisy sip from the Styrofoam cup he was holding.

Details of her kidnapping and rescue crept back into her memory. When she recalled the knife stab, she was thankful she didn't feel anything but tired. Tired and groggy. How much time had gone by? How long had she been passed out? She wiggled her fingers. Everything was working fine. Now she had to check her ...

"I can't move my feet." She hadn't meant to sound so panicked.

The detective cleared his throat. "Blame the anesthesia. The blade really couldn't have made a safer cut ..."

Kennedy looked around for something she could vomit into.

The detective stirred the coffee in his cup. "Now that you're awake, I have some questions to ask you."

"Beg your pardon, officer." Carl's tone was respectful, but his words were resolute. "She's just survived an abduction, a major injury ..."

Kennedy wasn't sure how Carl's retelling of all her recent trauma could help anything.

"What my husband is trying to say," Sandy jumped in, "is that maybe you could give her a little more time to recover. She just woke up not a minute ago. I imagine she wants to talk to her mom and dad ..."

Kennedy's throat constricted painfully at the mention of her parents.

The detective frowned. "Unfortunately, we have reason to believe that ..."

"I'll do it."

Three pairs of eyes stared down at her.

"I'll answer your questions." Kennedy still didn't feel like her tongue was working quite right, but they seemed to understand her.

"You don't have to," Sandy crooned. "Don't feel pressured ..."

"I already heard him make plans to kill somebody. A friend of Jodie's." She sucked in her breath. *Jodie*. She tried to sit up, but it was as if all her core muscles had gone on strike. "He sent Jodie to the hospital. She was passed out. He had tried to get her to take ..."

Detective Drikslay held up his hand. "We got the girl as soon as they came out of the complex. We were already there waiting."

"That was some fast thinking you did, contacting us on the church website." Carl was glowing as he stared down at her with his arm around his wife.

"We had plans to storm the complex for other reasons," the detective explained. "We would have jumped in with gas until we learned they were also holding hostages."

"What you did on that computer may have saved both of your lives," Sandy gushed.

Kennedy didn't care about any of this. "Where is Jodie now? Is she all right?"

"Your little friend will be just fine." The detective stared at his coffee, and Kennedy immediately noticed his use of the future tense. She looked to Carl and Sandy.

"She lost a lot of blood." Carl had such a different appearance when he wasn't smiling. "She's in another part of Providence right now getting a transfusion."

Kennedy detected the heaviness that seemed to crouch down on everyone's shoulders. She already knew the answer to her next question. "And the baby?"

Carl shook his head. "By the time she got here, it was too late."

"It was her uncle." Kennedy fixed her eyes on the detective, wondering if he was going to write that down on the little notepad in his breast pocket. "Anthony. He wanted to force her to have …"

"We know all about Anthony Abernathy." The detective scowled. "But I'm curious about what you said about killing someone."

Kennedy told him how Jodie didn't want her uncle to realize how far along in the pregnancy she really was. "Jodie said the boy wasn't really the father, but her uncle would think it was. She didn't want to get him in trouble. They mentioned a boys' home. Vermont, maybe?"

Detective Drisklay nodded. "We'll look into it."

Kennedy wanted to see Jodie. She wanted to hug her,

apologize for not finding a way to help her sooner. How much did one little girl have to endure? And then after she assured herself Jodie really was safe, Kennedy wanted to sleep for a very, very long time.

But she couldn't. Not now. There was still work to do. "Jodie's uncle told one of his men to go and ..." Could she bring herself to speak the words? "He told Dustin to go and kill that boy." Had she really just said that? Had it all really happened? If she weren't here lying in a hospital bed, if she didn't have such vivid memories of the cold, the hunger, the knife stab, she might have thought it was a dream that felt a little too real.

"Well, you don't have to worry about that," the detective assured her. "Anthony Abernathy and Dustin are dead. Killed on the scene."

Kennedy shut her eyes for a minute. Would she ever forget? Could she ever forget? "What about the other one? Vinny."

"He got away, but we suspect he's injured. The important thing is you're safe, and so is the girl."

"Her family knows by now?" Kennedy wondered how Wayne and Vivian Abernathy would respond to a crisis like this. What would it do to their picture-perfect family? She hoped Wayne would have the decency to stand up for his daughter instead of worrying how the events would impact his campaign, but she had her doubts.

"I just got back from praying with them." Carl sounded tired. "I think they're blaming themselves for what Anthony did. They never suspected."

"She was babysitting over there all the time," Sandy added. "They thought he just needed the extra help since Moriah died. They had no idea ..."

The detective cleared his throat, and Sandy took a step back. Kennedy tried to follow the gist of the conversation as he asked her more questions, but she never felt like she could grasp what was really going on. Her head felt as heavy as her calculus textbook when he finally left, mumbling something about sleeping off his coffee.

"I suppose we should be going, too." Carl helped Sandy into her sweater.

"What, so soon? I thought the party was just starting." The voice sounded familiar, but Kennedy couldn't place it until she saw the hair.

"Nick!" Sandy spread out her arms and gave him a hug. "That's nice of you to stop by."

He ran his hand through his dreads. "Well, I got Carl's text, and I figured I'd stop by right after youth group and see how everything's going." He gave Kennedy a little wave.

"How d'you feel?"

She was too tired to smile but tried to give him a reassuring nod. "I'll be just fine."

"You bet she will." Carl clapped Nick on the back.

Nick looked around the room awkwardly. He wore a bright orange Hawaiian shirt over a T-shirt with Jesus and his disciples all piled into a white Honda. The caption at the top read *In One Accord.* Kennedy probably would have been glad to see him if she weren't so exhausted. She wasn't certain she'd remember any of this in the morning. How long had it been since she had slept the whole night through?

"So the media is kinda going crazy over all this." Nick didn't seem to know where to focus his eyes, which darted from Carl to Sandy to the various objects lying around the room.

Sandy winced, but Nick went on with his explanation.

"I guess they're saying now Anthony Abernathy was on some sort of rampage. Trying to sabotage his brother's campaign."

Carl shrugged. "Everyone's desperate for a scoop."

"No, that's what he said before he ..." Kennedy swallowed. Had she really remembered right? She could still hear the shouts of her rescuers and the sound of gunfire when she shut her eyes. Her whole body sank farther into her hospital mattress at the thought of Jodie and all she had gone through.

"I still don't know how someone so close to Wayne could do a thing like that," Sandy breathed.

"That appears to be the question of the day." Nick put one foot up on a little hospital chair near the wall and drummed on his bent knee. "Some are guessing it has more to do with protecting his own hide than anything else."

Carl made a motion to the door. "Maybe we should talk about this more on our way out."

"That's a good idea," Sandy replied.

Nick offered a sheepish good-bye. Kennedy wanted to tell them she didn't mind. She was dying to understand it all herself. But her vision grew blurry as she watched them gather up their things, and she was asleep before their voices died out in the hall.

CHAPTER 26

A nurse came in sometime in the middle of the night and recorded Kennedy's vitals. Whatever medicines they had given her were starting to wear off, and she itched and tried to get comfortable for another hour before dozing off again. In the morning, a nurse checked her bandages one last time and told her she would get her discharge papers ready. "Your pastor said he'd come pick you up in about an hour."

Kennedy wondered what it would be like to go back to the real world after an ordeal like this. Would she ever feel safe on the streets of Cambridge again? Would she ever feel safe in her own dorm? She thought about the pregnancy center, about the big Thursday dinner that would go on as if none of this had happened. Could people really go on living in such blissful ignorance? She couldn't. Like an over-stretched rubber band that can never resume its original shape, she couldn't close her eyes again and forget it all.

Her dad would tell her he had been right all along, of

course. He would probably chide her for following Dustin the night he came to her room. Kennedy had been worried about Willow, that was all. And her compassion could have killed her. She wouldn't mind, though. Her dad could rage for an hour as long as Kennedy could hear his voice. As long as she could sit with the phone to her ear and listen to that strong, familiar, lecturing tone. All the homesickness of the past two months collected itself into one massive swell that came crashing down with tsunami-like force all around her. It wasn't like drowning. It was like being hit by a ten-foot brick wall.

"Excuse me. Do I have the right room?"

Kennedy squinted at the man in the doorway.

He smiled. "So here you are. Remember me?"

There was something familiar about that red hair. The guy from the subway. The journalist. What was he doing here? He gave her a casual smile and strode to her bedside.

"I saw your picture come up on my news feed. I never forget a face." He held up his camera case.

Oh no. Was he here for pictures, then?

Kennedy raised the back of her hospital bed so she was sitting up. At least she was in her street clothes already. What was he doing here? She wasn't sure if she should be talking to the media at all. Or was that only what they told victims in novels?

"I'm not here to interview you or anything." He patted his bag and kept it closed.

Kennedy stared. So he was a mind-reader, too? Or was he just used to people not trusting him because he was with the press? "It's just that I don't meet too many young people from Jilin Province. And, well, I guess when I saw you were involved in all this, I wanted to check in. Make sure you were all right."

His endearing smile only took away a fraction of Kennedy's misgivings.

He sighed. "Well, what do the doctors say?" He eyed her hospital room with a calculating, meticulous care. Was he some kind of Sherlock Holmes? What could his trained eye learn about her condition simply by observing her surroundings?

"I'll be just fine. Maybe a week or two of taking it easy. You know, after I catch up on all the homework I missed."

He crossed his arms. A little dimple dented his right cheek when he smiled. "I was a lot like that my first year, too."

She didn't ask him what he meant. She thought she was already learning.

He shook his head. "So you probably heard Anthony

Abernathy was shot."

A shudder started in the base of her back and sped up her spine. She winced when it reached the spot of her injury.

"They're saying he did it because of his wife."

Kennedy felt her face scrunch up in about a dozen unasked questions.

He leaned forward. "Moriah Abernathy? Did you guys hear about her over there in Yanji?"

The name sounded vaguely familiar, but Kennedy couldn't place it.

"Anyway, she was pregnant when they diagnosed her with aggressive cancer. She refused chemo. No abortion, either. She died a few weeks after her son was born."

"Charlie."

"Pardon?"

Kennedy shook her head. "Never mind. So this is all some sort of vengeance because his wife died?"

He tightened the strap of his camera case. "I guess he figures if she hadn't gotten so much pressure from the pro-life camp, his wife wouldn't have been so adamant. Maybe she would've gotten the medical care she needed."

Kennedy wondered if it was the exhaustion or the pain meds that were most responsible for fogging up her brain.

He leaned forward. "Between you and me, there's chatter

about other motives for hiding the girl's pregnancy, too. Selfish ones. Meant to hide incriminating evidence, if you catch my drift."

Kennedy squinted. Did he mean what she thought he meant? And if so, was she really surprised?

"But that's all spec at this point. You know how it is."

No, she didn't, but she wasn't going to tell him so.

He leaned against the end table by her bed. "You hear about the computer they recovered?"

She still hadn't figured out if this was an interview or some strange and unexpected courtesy call. If it was an interview, he was revealing lots and gleaning hardly anything, at least nothing she was giving him verbally. What was it her dad always said about Kennedy trusting strangers?

"I guess it had all kinds of incriminating evidence," he went on. "Wayne Abernathy's itinerary, blueprints of his election headquarters. Sounds like they were also planning to target some pro-life fundraiser later on this week."

Kennedy couldn't keep her poker face and felt her eyes grow wide. "But they stopped it?"

He shrugged. "As far as I know. I'm sure they'll have extra security just in case. You might want to tell your pastor to plan for more guests."

A nurse bustled in before Kennedy could figure out how

he knew so much about her and about the whole situation. "I'll have to ask you to leave," she told the reporter. "We have some discharge directions from the doctor to discuss."

He cracked another wide smile, his dimple pierced his cheek, and he was gone before Kennedy learned his name. She had a hard time focusing while the nurse went over all the paperwork. She wished she could go home to her parents for a long weekend. Why couldn't they live closer?

The nurse left, and Kennedy reached over for the Bible on her nightstand. Had someone left if for her there? She couldn't remember seeing it last night, but she had been so drugged up and exhausted she could have missed anything. There was a note inside the front cover.

To Kennedy ~ Psalm 139.

Psalm 139. It sounded like a passage she should be familiar with. The pages crinkled as she turned them.

You have searched me, Lord, and you know me. How many times in Yanji had she ached for God to show himself to her, for him to let her know he cared for her, not only the missionaries and evangelists of the world?

You know when I sit and when I rise. She looked back on the past thirty-six hours. The whole time, God had known where she was. He had a plan to rescue her all along.

You perceive my going out and my lying down. You are

familiar with all my ways. Her life, as isolated and lonely as it had felt for the past few months in the States, was an open book her heavenly Father had memorized. There wasn't a lab write-up, a calculus problem, a late-night snack of dry Cheerios that he didn't know about. And he loved her.

Kennedy was only halfway through the Psalm when Carl nudged open the door carrying a colorful bouquet of flowers and brandishing a huge smile. "Grab your things. Sandy insists you spend the next few days with us while you recover."

Kennedy wanted to argue. She wanted to tell him that she needed to get back to her dorm, back to her classes. She couldn't even guess how far behind she already was. But the dull ache in her back had grown exponentially since she woke up until she was sure she could feel Anthony behind her, stabbing her in the same spot repeatedly whenever she shifted her position. The doctor had assured her it would get better and ordered her to rest. Well, there wasn't time for that. Not with labs and calculus and *Crime and Punishment* …

"She's already baking you muffins." Carl rolled a hospital wheelchair to the side of the bed. "She said the food back in your dorm won't heal you up half as fast as her home cooking." He reached his hand out and helped her down.

"You ready?"

There was no point arguing. "Yeah." Once in the wheelchair, Kennedy put the new Bible on her lap. She had to swallow twice before she could trust her voice again. "I'm ready."

CHAPTER 27

Kennedy spent that day resting on the Lindgrens' couch, napping in their guest room, and assuring her mother over a series of five different phone conversations that she really was safe and unharmed. She nibbled her breakfast, finished about half of her lunch, and by evening was so hungry she cleaned her dinner plate twice.

Kennedy got in touch with her professors and wasn't expected back in class until Monday. She had some work to do in the meantime to keep from falling too far behind, but Carl and Sandy insisted she stay at their home through the end of the weekend. Kennedy surprised herself and didn't protest.

On Thursday morning, Sandy drove Kennedy over to her dorm so she could pick up her books. The door to her room was slightly open. Kennedy's body shook at the memory of what had happened the last time she was there.

"So, our little celebrity finally makes her grand stage debut." Willow's face lit up when they entered, and she stood up from her desk. Her hair was already a darker shade than it had been at the beginning of the week. She took a step toward Kennedy. "I'm like not gonna injure you if I give you a hug or something, will I?"

Kennedy blinked. Her dad had ordered her a new set of contacts that would arrive in the mail in a week or less. "No, just be gentle." She smiled. It was the first time she and Willow touched each other, at least as far as she could remember.

"So, you selling your book rights yet or anything?"

Kennedy winced at the shouts and gunshots bursting from Willow's computer game.

"Oh, sorry about that." Willow reached out and shut the monitor off.

Kennedy looked around. Besides Willow's hair color, nothing had changed. There were her books on the shelf, her bag on the floor. She could tell by one of the lights that her laptop hadn't even been shut down properly. Her phone — the real one, not the clone — was right there on her desk where she had left it.

"Do you want me to pick out a few outfits for you to bring back with us?" Sandy asked.

Kennedy had forgotten Sandy was there. "That would be great." So far, she had been wearing Sandy's old house dresses, which were comfortable enough on her back but not exactly what she'd consider her own personal style. She had already seen the way Willow raised her eyebrows at the oversized floral thing she was wearing today. "By the way, Sandy, this is my roommate Willow. This is Sandy, my pastor's wife."

She half-expected Willow to go into some tirade about the horrors of organized religion, but Willow simply waved her hand and gave her stage-ready smile. Kennedy pointed out the books she'd need, and Sandy packed them in a little duffel. To Kennedy's surprise, Willow remained where she was instead of plopping back down behind her computer. "So you skipping town or something? Going into witness protection?"

Kennedy laughed. "No. I'm just going to be staying at Sandy's for another few days until I'm recovered."

"Well, I know you're going to be wicked busy because you're a huge over-achiever that way, but you need to make time for me to take you to the L'Aroma Bakery so you can tell me everything that happened. You know, before your memoir hits the bookshelves and everything."

Kennedy wasn't sure if Willow was being sarcastic or not, but she could sense the genuine concern behind the words. "Yeah, I'd like that." It might be a while before she was ready to talk about it all, but she was glad Willow would be there to listen when the time came.

"Oh, by the way, your boyfriend's been stopping by … I don't know, like every other hour to see if you're back. He said he's called you a dozen times or something, but your phone battery must've died. Again."

Kennedy felt Sandy's curious stare at the mention of the word *boyfriend*. Well, even though they weren't dating, it was sweet that Reuben was so worried about her. She made herself a mental note to call him back at the Lindgrens'.

Sandy refused to let Kennedy carry any of her things back to the car. As soon as they were on the road, Sandy stole a quick sideways glance. *"Boyfriend?"*

Kennedy tried to keep her voice casual. "He's just a good friend. My lab partner."

"Just a friend?" Sandy asked with that same playful tone. "Just a friend that stops by every hour on the hour to see if you're ok?"

Kennedy felt the smile creep up on her face before she could stop it. Part of her wanted to change the subject. Part of her looked forward to getting her phone charged and hearing Reuben's easy-going voice and cool accent again.

Sandy put on some worship music, and they drove for a while without saying anything. Kennedy didn't know how she could ever show her full appreciation to the Lindgrens for everything they'd done for her. She wished she didn't have to have this next conversation, but she may as well get over it. It wasn't going to get any easier later.

"You know, I've been meaning to tell you and Carl ..."

Sandy reached over and lowered the speaker volume.

"I think I'm going to put my volunteer work on hold."

Sandy turned a corner. "Well, that's fine by us. We figured you may need time off after all you went through."

"It's not just that." Could Sandy ever begin to guess what was going on in Kennedy's heart? Kennedy hated to acknowledge it even to herself, but there was no way she was worthy to rejoin the pro-life movement. Not now. Probably not ever. As they drove, Kennedy told Sandy about the doubts that had plagued her since she took the first call from Jodie. "I just don't really know where I stand on abortion at this point. I know it's wrong. I know it's taking an innocent life. But, I mean, what about someone like Jodie? She's so tiny. I don't think her body would have been able to carry a baby to term, and even if she could, I wouldn't have wished that on her."

Sandy was quiet. Kennedy expected her to come back with a Bible verse or a pro-life platitude to cover over all of Kennedy's doubts and uncertainties like a miniature Band-Aid. The silence was unnerving, so she kept talking.

"There was a point when I realized they wanted to give Jodie the abortion pills, and a little part of me was sad that she was too far along in the pregnancy to actually take them. I mean, wouldn't that be infinitely easier on her body?"

"Easier?" Sandy repeated, and Kennedy stared out the passenger window.

"I don't know. I just, I wanted Jodie to be safe." She was shaking. Could Sandy tell? The singer on the radio crooned quietly about God's glorious majesty, and all Kennedy could think about was the puddle of blood on the floor of that bathroom.

She waited for Sandy to respond, for her to tell her that it was normal to doubt. It was normal to feel the way she did. But Sandy only turned another corner and said, "We have one more quick stop." It wasn't until Kennedy saw the blue signs on the side of the road that she realized where they were headed.

When they parked in front of Providence Hospital, Kennedy's legs refused to move. *I can't do this*, she wanted to say, but she couldn't find the breath to form the words.

Sandy put her hand on top of Kennedy's. "There's someone here who's been asking to see you."

Two silent tears streaked unchecked down Kennedy's cheeks.

Sandy insisted they borrow one of the hospital's wheelchairs since Jodie was staying in the children's section, two towers over and four stories up. Kennedy and Sandy made their way through hallways painted in bright primary colors, watched a clown performing for a few dozen kids in hospital gowns, and passed dozens of patient rooms, but they still reached their destination before Kennedy was ready.

"Are you all right?" Sandy asked.

Kennedy blinked her eyes, and Sandy rolled the wheelchair in.

A nurse was busy adjusting some funny gadgets on Jodie's feet. She looked even smaller in her hospital gown. A shy smile inched its way across her face. "Hi."

Kennedy sniffed. "Hi."

Sandy wheeled the chair right up to the bedside. The nurse silently excused herself, and Sandy exclaimed loudly, "You know, I've been needing to find a restroom since we left the house. I'll be back."

Kennedy had no idea what to say. One of Jodie's arms was bruised near the indent of her elbow. The other had an IV hooked up to it. Her face was puffy, but she looked stronger and had better color. She was sitting up in her bed and looked as embarrassed and unsure of herself as Kennedy felt.

"How ..."

"Did you ..."

They both began at once, and both stopped at the same time with nervous chuckles.

"How are you?" Kennedy finally asked. Their voices were hushed, as if Dustin and Vinny were right outside the door, listening in on everything they said.

"I ended up needing surgery. They ..." Jodie swallowed and stared at her Curious George sheets. "They, um, they said I'll be able to go home in a few more days."

"That's great news." Kennedy tried to sound positive but knew she had failed.

"I'm glad they got you out safe," Jodie said. "My dad told me as soon as he heard."

"Me, too." Kennedy tried to swallow. "I ... Well, you were really sick. I was happy to hear you made it to the hospital."

They stared blankly, and a few seconds later they both let out another round of nervous laughs, still under their breaths, still hushed, still haunted by the memories they both shared.

"You probably need your rest," Kennedy finally stated. When would Sandy get back? Why had she ditched her here?

"Yeah, my mom's been sleeping with me at night. Oh!" Jodie's eyes widened. "Did you hear? It looks like we'll probably be able to adopt Charlie."

Kennedy forced a smile. "That's great news." As hard as she tried, she couldn't drag any degree of enthusiasm into her voice.

"Yeah." Jodie's expression fell flat again by degrees. "I was really glad to hear that. He was fine, by the way. The day I was babysitting, I mean. He was fine. The police found him at his grandma's." She cleared her throat.

Kennedy glanced at the clock. How long was Sandy going to take?

"You know about my uncle?"

The question caught Kennedy off guard. Was Jodie asking if she knew he was dead? Or something else? She nodded tentatively.

Jodie let out her breath. "The doctor said something about giving the baby a DNA test. I guess you can do that even after ... Well ..." She bit her lower lip and stared past Kennedy. "At least Samir won't get in trouble. Once they get the results back, I mean."

"So it really was ...?" Kennedy couldn't bring herself to complete the thought.

Jodie let out what sounded like a bad imitation of a laugh. "I didn't want to tell my parents, you know, because I thought it might hurt the election."

Kennedy didn't know what to say. From their first phone conversation, there had been a connection, a certain camaraderie between her and Jodie she couldn't explain. Now, she felt like they were slipping apart, pulled away from each other by a gravity far too strong for either to resist.

"It was a boy, you know." Jodie's voice was a small hush.

Kennedy felt her face scrunch up awkwardly. The corners of her eyes felt warm.

"A little, tiny baby boy," Jodie breathed, staring past Kennedy's shoulder.

"I bet he was beautiful." Kennedy tried to cough but ended up making a painful choking noise deep in the back of her throat.

"I told my mom …" Jodie let out her breath nervously. "I told my mom I wanted a picture. He just, he was so perfect. Do you think that's weird?"

Kennedy shook her head but couldn't form any words.

"I decided to name him Wayne."

Kennedy tried to say she thought it was a perfect name, but she wasn't sure she got it out right.

"They even let me hold him for a minute or two. I talked to him. Just a little. I told him I was sorry for thinking about, well, you know. I told him I hoped he wouldn't forget me."

She looked over at Kennedy with shining eyes. "I want him to remember me when I get to heaven. Because when I'm there, I know I'm going to recognize him right away. Don't you think?"

Kennedy didn't know who started crying first. She didn't know who reached out for whom. But when Sandy came to the door, Kennedy was up on Jodie's bed. They were curled up into each other's arms and sobbing, mourning little Wayne, releasing all the fear and trauma of the past few days. Kennedy cried for both of their lost innocence, for the depravity that made such a sweet child suffer unimaginable torment, for the cruelty that spilled over into a world Kennedy had previously assumed was safe.

Sandy caught Kennedy's eye and pointed to the hallway, mouthing, *I'll be out here.* Half an hour later when their tears were dried up, Jodie said her mom would stop by with Charlie to visit soon. She and Kennedy both chuckled a little again as they said good-bye, and then Kennedy let Sandy wheel her back to the car. They didn't say anything on the way home, but the silence filled Kennedy's wounded, weary soul like words never could.

CHAPTER 28

As soon as they got back to the Lindgrens', Kennedy took her pain meds and went to the guest room to lie down. Carl and Sandy would be busy that afternoon getting ready for the pregnancy center's big dinner. It would be Wayne Abernathy's first public statement since his daughter's kidnapping. They had to make a last-minute room change because even St. Margaret's huge fellowship hall wasn't large enough to accommodate both the guests and the press who would be there. Nick recruited a bunch of kids from the youth group to stop by after school to set up tables in the sanctuary. There would be extra security too, although everyone assumed with Anthony dead and the computer confiscated the attacks wouldn't proceed as planned.

"You're welcome to come with us." Carl took a noisy slurp of soup that Sandy had whipped together for a late lunch.

"I'll see how much reading I get done this afternoon." Kennedy was glad when Carl didn't push the issue any further. The thought of being there with so many people left her paralyzed.

When the time came to set up the church, Carl asked Kennedy again if she wanted to come. "If you're not ready now, one of us could swing by and pick you up a little before six. No problem."

Sandy laid her hand on her husband's shoulder. "I think she needs to rest."

In this case, Kennedy was happy to let Sandy answer for her.

"Well, just text us if you change your mind," Carl called out as he went to the bedroom to hunt for his lost keys.

Once the Lindgrens left, it was the first time Kennedy was alone since the kidnapping. She hobbled around to make sure both the front and back doors were locked. She wasn't in the mood to read, and *Crime and Punishment* wasn't the right kind of book for a day like this anyway. Her usual spy or thriller novels wouldn't be the right kind of distraction, either. Would she be stuck reading historical romances like her mom for the rest of her life? She heated up a bread roll Sandy left for her, glanced at some of her reading for her general chemistry class, and tried to remember where she had put that Bible someone had left her in the hospital. She found it a minute later in the guest room and returned to Psalm 139.

For you created my inmost being; you knit me together in my mother's womb. Kennedy sat staring at the words. Shouldn't they speak to her? Shouldn't they mean something at a time like this?

I praise you because I am fearfully and wonderfully made. What did Jodie's baby look like? She almost wished Jodie had offered to show her the picture she had. Was he a tiny version of his mother? Kennedy tried to swallow away the lump in her throat with another bite of bread.

When I was woven together in the depths of the earth, your eyes saw my unformed body. God had loved that baby. She knew now that Jodie had, too. Was that what pastors and politicians meant when they spouted off terms like *sanctity of life?*

All the days ordained for me were written in your book before one of them came to be. All the days. Did that include baby Wayne's days in the womb? Had he been knitted together in time to know how much God loved him? To know how much his mom loved him, scared and young and ill-prepared as she was?

Kennedy's eyes hurt. She shut the Bible and thought

about calling Reuben. She wasn't quite sure why she hadn't yet. Part of her was scared he would ask too many questions. Another part of her didn't want to admit anything had changed. She didn't want to talk. Especially about the past few days.

Kennedy checked her phone. Tomorrow, Carl would take it in to get the surveillance bugs removed. Did she really want to use it yet? She stared at her empty plate and her assignment notebook for another twenty minutes before she finally picked it back up and found Reuben's name in her contacts.

"It's about time I heard from you!" There was both relief and good humor in his voice.

Kennedy couldn't help laughing. "I'm sorry. It's been a busy few days."

"I'm sure it has. I'm hearing all about it right now, actually."

"What do you mean?"

"Check out Channel 7 News and then call me back."

Kennedy wasn't sure she wanted to hear some newscaster recount the horrid details of her and Jodie's capture. She was sure they wouldn't spare Jodie any courtesies on account of her age. She knew Carl had been right. Anything that might stink of scandal this close to the election was going to make huge headlines.

Reuben had already ended the call. She didn't want to spend the rest of the night in such suffocating silence, and she knew Reuben would probably want to know how many details from the news report were accurate. Part of her wondered the same thing. Fortunately, the Lindgrens' TV was one of the old-fashioned kinds that were really easy to use. She flipped to channel 7 and saw Wayne Abernathy's face instead of the floating head she expected. The news ticker at the bottom flashed details about Jodie's capture and child-abuse allegations against the late Anthony Abernathy, but Kennedy was paying too much attention to Wayne's speech to try to read them all.

"I've been the front-line man when it comes to the war against abortion for some time now. It's a cause I believe in deeply, a cause I've fought for zealously." He was wearing a red, white, and blue tie and one of those little American flag lapel pins. Fitting for a pre-election speech.

"Unfortunately, my commitment to the pro-life movement has had a price, a price my wife, our children, and our extended family have had to pay. Last year, many of you blessed us with your condolences, prayers, and well-wishes when my sister-in-law passed away. Moriah was a beautiful, angelic creature, who chose to delay chemotherapy treatment when she discovered she was pregnant. Her choice was a personal one, not forced upon her by any pastor or priest or politician. It was a choice her doctors may have disagreed with, but they respected it as a choice that she alone could make."

Kennedy leaned forward to listen.

"Moriah died shortly after giving the precious gift of life to my little nephew, Charlie. Our memories of her will be of a woman who was strong, courageous, who found strength in God and wasn't afraid of dying. Everyone who knew her suffered when she passed, but none more than her husband."

Wayne cleared his throat. He would probably make a good actor. Kennedy could picture him on stage next to Willow.

"I'm sure most of you by now have heard of the charges and allegations brought against my brother, Anthony. Charges of vandalizing the new Cambridge Community Pregnancy Center, whose opening we celebrate tonight. Charges of targeting my campaign in order to stop the pro-life cause in our state. And, unfortunately, charges that hit much closer to home."

Kennedy turned up the volume so she wouldn't miss a word.

"My daughter, as you have already heard, was pregnant

when she was abducted Tuesday morning. It was as much as a shock to us as it was to you, believe me. Unfortunately, Anthony learned about the pregnancy before we did and tried to convince our daughter to kill her unborn baby. He eventually resorted to kidnapping her with the intention of forcing an abortion. We assume it was an attempt to smear my campaign. Any motivations beyond that are purely speculation at this point, and I ask that in deference to our family's privacy and to our daughter's young age that none of us allow the spread of ungrounded, malicious rumors."

Staring past the blinding, dazzling spotlights and camera flashes, Kennedy was surprised at how many wrinkles were on Wayne's face. Not something she noticed the other times she had seen him.

"I would like to publically thank God as well as the FBI team who responded at the rescue scene to ensure my daughter and the other hostage involved were delivered to safety. Unfortunately, injuries sustained during my daughter's abduction resulted in a spontaneous miscarriage. Please note that this was not the result of an elective abortion, and that if her mother and I had known about her condition ..." Here his voice caught. He took a drink of bottled water. "We would have done everything in our power to give our daughter a safe and healthy pregnancy. We would have opened our arms and our home to give our grandson a loving, caring childhood. I would also like to take this chance to publically announce that even if our daughter had gone through with the abortion procedure like her uncle wanted, we would have loved her unconditionally, just as God loves his own children."

Kennedy's throat was parched, but she didn't want to get up for a drink. Not yet.

"Because of these recent events, I have decided to withdraw from the gubernatorial race next week. My priority right now is to be with my family, to ensure my daughter gets the rest and healing she needs, and to protect our privacy during this difficult time. My wife and I have also assumed guardianship of my nephew, Charlie, and we will be busy helping him adjust to life without either his father or his mother. For those of you inclined to prayer, I ask you to remember us."

The next few minutes were filled with questions from the press and comments from the newscaster, who was a little zealous in reporting that one of the kidnapping suspects was still at large. Kennedy finally turned the TV off, wincing as she stood up from the couch. Her back was stiff. She thought she could use a hot shower but wasn't sure she had the energy to move down the hall.

There was a knock on the door. Kennedy froze.

"Kennedy? You in there?" Her heart raced as fast as spinning electrons. She grabbed her phone, ready to call 911. "Kennedy?"

If she could slow down her heart to remember where she had heard the voice before ...

"It's me, Nick. From St. Margaret's."

Kennedy shuffled toward the door, still not sure how she felt about the intrusion into her evening of solitude. "Hi." She held the door open but couldn't mask the question in her voice. Nick looked halfway normal in khaki pants and a dark blue sweater. He could have passed for any one of Cambridge's thousands of young men in casual work attire if it hadn't been for the dreadlocks. What was he doing here?

"Carl sent me. He says they have way too much food, and he wants you to come get your fill." Nick lowered his voice. "But Sandy wants you to know it's totally fine if you stay home and rest. She'll make sure Carl doesn't give you a hard time for it."

Kennedy thought about all the schoolwork she had to catch up on. She thought about Reuben, who was probably expecting her to call him right back. Was she ready to return to St. Margaret's? To the pregnancy center? She thought about her former resolve to distance herself from the pro-life movement, thought about the time she spent with Jodie in the hospital, the tears they shed over baby Wayne, the verses she had read a few minutes earlier. Did she know how she felt about abortion now? It was still wrong, but when she tried to articulate why, all she could picture was baby Wayne as he must have looked in Jodie's arms. Was that enough? It would have to be, at least for now.

She offered Nick an uncertain smile. "Let's go."

She reached to grab her coat off its hanger, but Nick stopped her. "Let me help you with that." She was glad to not have to twist herself into it.

The phone rang. "Can I meet you at the car?" she asked Nick. "This will only take me a minute or two."

"Sure thing. I'll take your bag and meet you there."

Kennedy didn't even look at the caller ID before she answered. "Hey, Reuben."

"That was some crazy story."

Would she ever be able to look back over the past few days without shaking? "Yeah, sure was."

"You ok?" His words were laden with concern.

"I'm really tired. My stitches are itching, too."

"Ouch. When are you coming back to campus?"

"This weekend sometime. I should be moving around a

lot easier by then."

"Can I get you something? Heating pads? Pain meds?"

Kennedy let out her breath. It was good to hear his voice. "How about the notes from today's chemistry lecture?"

"Consider it done."

They talked for another minute about nothing important and made plans for Reuben to stop by the Lindgrens' tomorrow evening with his lecture notes. Kennedy warned him to come with his appetite since Sandy would almost certainly force him to stay for dinner.

They hung up, and Kennedy zipped up her coat. As she locked up Carl and Sandy's house behind her, she thought about tomorrow, and peace wrapped itself around her like a warm blanket. She was glad Reuben hadn't asked for any more details about the kidnapping. It was therapeutic somehow to talk about something as mundane as school.

Kennedy limped down the driveway and balked when she saw Nick standing in front of a VW bus that looked about as old as her dad. "You actually drive this?"

He grinned and held the passenger door open. "It's the youth group van, actually. I prefer my bike, but I didn't think you'd be up for a ten-mile ride."

She chuckled, even though the movement shot pain through her back muscles and made her cringe. "Yeah, maybe not."

He tapped the hood, which had a painted picture of a tie-dye Jesus fish about to swallow up a cartoon-style shark. "What do you think?"

Kennedy was too overwhelmed by so many colors to form a personal opinion. "Is that Michelangelo?" She pointed to a picture of a Ninja Turtle surfing with a Bible in one hand.

"Nah. Donatello. I was going to make it Jesus, but Carl pulled the senior pastor card on me and said it would be irreverent." He tapped the windshield. "I did get the Peter, James, and John bobble-head set, though. You can see it better once we're inside."

"So you did all this yourself?" Kennedy eyed the sunset scene painted on the passenger side. Looking closer, she saw the individual Bible verses stenciled in to form the branches of a palm tree.

"Like it?" he beamed.

"It suits you well," was all she could manage.

Once she was inside the bus, Nick handed her the seatbelt and shut her in. She thought about Reuben, about her calculus test, about the mounds of homework she would tackle starting tomorrow. After everything she had already been through, would she ever get stressed out over a test again?

Yes, she probably would. Life would turn back to normal, she'd get caught up in her studies, and in a month, a semester, maybe a year, she'd wonder if anything could be more nerve-racking than having two tests, a paper, and a lab all due in the same week. She would never forget Jodie or the time they spent together in that basement, but she didn't have to relive that moment every day of her life. As Nick drove to St. Margaret's, the future opened out before her like a brand-new novel with limitless possibilities for adventure, blessings, and growth between its covers.

She couldn't wait to see what the next chapter would contain.

ACKNOWLEDGEMENTS

With every book I write, I become even more convinced that I couldn't pen a single sentence if the Lord wasn't the one sustaining me. I am so thankful to him for fulfilling my lifelong dream to be an author. While I am writing, my body, mind, and spirit constantly remind me how weak I am. While I worked on *Unplanned*, it was the Lord who soothed my eyestrain and alleviated the symptoms of carpal tunnel so I could complete this story, and I am so thankful.

My husband sacrifices countless hours giving advice and letting me bounce ideas off him. I thank God for his support, and for the fact that he doesn't complain when my compulsive pacing makes him dizzy.

I have been so blessed to work with Sheila Hollinghead on several of my novels now, and she deserves a huge shout-out, not just for her thorough edits, but for her willingness to work at lightning speed this round. Thank you, Sheila, as well as Annie Lima Douglass for her proofs.

I'd also like to say a big thank you to the bloggers, reviewers, readers, and friends who gave me feedback on the early drafts of *Unplanned*, and a special thank you goes out to the members of my prayer team, who really did pray this book into existence.

There were some questions I ran into while writing *Unplanned* that Google just couldn't help me with. I'm thankful for Liz Worman, an OB nurse and friend who answered some of my pregnancy-related medical questions; Bob Baldwin, a fellow Christian author and EMT who gave feedback about Kennedy's knife wound; Bill Donovan, a Christian suspense writer who also leads a pregnancy care center; and Zack Kullis, who works for the FBI and has experience in hostage rescue. I am thankful to each of you for taking the time to answer the many strange and random questions I threw out at you.

When I was a brand-new volunteer at our local pregnancy center, I received a call much like the one Kennedy receives from Rose. I never did find out who the girl was or find a way to help her, but this book is dedicated to her. I hope God has blessed you with a beautiful, peaceful, glorious life knowing and loving just how much He loves you.

If you are a young reader and happen to find yourself in a situation even remotely similar to Jodie's, please know that you are not alone. Find someone you can talk to, like your parents, another family member, a teacher, school counselor, pastor, etc. If at any age you need help making decisions about an unplanned pregnancy, see if your community has a pregnancy center or visit www.lifecall.org to email, text, or call someone willing to listen to your story.

Last of all, if you have had an abortion and want to learn more about post-abortion syndrome, you can read testimonies of those who have found healing and wholeness after abortions at ramahinternational.org. Many local pregnancy centers also offer free, non-judgmental post-abortion counseling.

Want more from Alana Terry?

Check out **www.alanaterry.com** for current titles.

Sign up to get emails with each new release at

www.alanaterry.com/newsletter

DISCUSSION
QUESTIONS

The following questions can be for personal reflection or for use with a book club. *Please note: If you are facilitating a discussion about* Unplanned, *please remember that many Christian women have had abortions, and just because somebody is a Christian doesn't guarantee they are pro-life. In case you don't know if your group is ready to handle such heavy topics, I have placed all of the abortion-related questions in their own separate subheading. Feel free to skip these (or any other questions you find here) at your discretion.*

General Questions

1. When was the first time you called 911 or your country's equivalent emergency response number?

2. Have you spent much time in a foreign country? How did that experience shape you?

3. Have you ever experienced culture shock?

4. What were you like at the age of eighteen? Were you an overachiever like Kennedy, a free spirit like Willow, calm and collected like Reuben, or something else?

5. How many times did you move houses before you graduated high school?

6. When you were a teen, did you think your parents were overprotective like Kennedy does? If you are a parent, how protective would you say you are?

7. If you were to go back to school today, what would you want to study?

8. What was the hardest adjustment you had to make when you first started living on your own?

9. If you had four spare hours a week where you could volunteer anywhere, what would you do?

10. Have you ever been in Kennedy's situation when you really wanted to help somebody but were powerless to do so?

11. Could you relate to Kennedy when she went to St. Margaret's for the first time? Do you ever feel disconnected at your church? How does your church do at welcoming newcomers?

12. Describe a time when you felt God's comfort and peace like Kennedy eventually does after she's captured.

13. Have you ever had an experience like Kennedy's when it felt like God wasn't answering any of your prayers at all?

14. Who is a politician or other public figure that you respect and admire?

Abortion-Specific Questions

Please note, some of these questions are written with the assumption that most people who read Unplanned *are at least sympathetic to the pro-life movement. If you are leading a discussion with a group of readers from different political backgrounds, you might want to focus just on questions 1 - 4 or skip this section altogether. The purpose of* Unplanned *is to foster healthy discussion, not to cause political rifts.*

1. What are the primary reasons pro-lifers give for being pro-life?

2. What are the primary reasons pro-abortionists give for being pro-abortion?

3. Wayne Abernathy says he doesn't have a right to be involved in pro-life ministry if he isn't willing to help single moms. Do you agree or disagree?

4. What kind of practical support do pregnant teens or single moms need? Who is a person, church, or organization you know of that is doing this well?

5. Fill in the blank. "The best way to end abortion is _____."

6. "If we want abortions to stop, we must stop judging women who get pregnant out of wedlock." Do you agree with this statement?

7. How would you counsel someone considering abortion if she is very young like Jodie?

8. How would you counsel someone considering abortion if she is in danger of dying herself if she carries the baby to term like Jodie's aunt?

Books by Alana Terry

North Korea Christian Suspense Novels

The Beloved Daughter

Slave Again

Torn Asunder

Flower Swallow

Kennedy Stern Christian Suspense Series

Unplanned

Paralyzed

Policed

Straightened

Turbulence

See a full list at www.alanaterry.com

Made in United States
Troutdale, OR
01/19/2024

16986426R00176